Travels with Lovers

STEVE DREBEN

PUBLISHED 3Y FIDELI PUBLISHING, INC.

Table of Contents

THE TOWER

The Tower

The hours were becoming hard. At first it was all easy, everything the way it was supposed to be everything fell into a perfect trove, nothing different, nothing changed or out of place. Then there was a shift, hours altered, hours changed…all the years given, all the years… perfect service the way it was supposed be…and then more change… liked the way it was… period. Everything had been in excellent order, and from there it began to change again…a flood of continuous shifts… even our marriage.

Brenda and I had been married thirteen years — we had word order, home order…our lives in perfect order. …Both of us loved order and Brenda was my exact duplicate in that arena. She was almost perfection as a wife and friend. … We shared a love for Roman history, especially the period from 200 A.D.-300 A.D.

Brenda was like a senator's wife who worked to build something together in the republic. I remembered how we'd gone to Reno or Las Vegas to see the UFC and professional boxing matches…this was during the last parts of our marriage…what a perfect escort she was ..she enjoyed all of it. Long stays in good hotels, baths together, and we'd party together all night. … Funny how much we enjoyed each other — it was so unique for these times.

Now every day pulled at me, assigned to *the tower* ...every step up to it reminded me of Brenda, or what we had together — serving her breakfast in bed with a flower, how she loved that. Eggs with a little sausage patty and some golden sliced potatoes on the side...and the smell, mixed with hers, was wonderful. I'd ask, "Did you enjoy those peppered potatoes? Weren't they wonderful?"

"Yes, they were cooked perfectly, Frank, and you're just so sweet to me, always know what I want. ... You always seem to know that, Frank. You always seem to know."

Now I sit alone — always alone — watching television at night. Always with a beer, and maybe some sloppy sandwich — alone, always alone. Brenda's gone somewhere — run away — maybe back to her family in Southern Illinois. Only been there once...just once.

I always thought of her coming up the tower steps — thought about what we had. ... Seems like I never really knew it at all, until she was gone. I guess that's the way it is between a man and a woman — never really understanding what you have until it's gone.

Nothing in my life ever seemed out of place, nothing was anything but plain normal. I enjoyed the routine "the sameness" — the habit, the unchanged. ... I knew what I wanted since I was a child. My mother always told me how easy a child I was ... how I'd always "kept to the path," never wavered...kept courage, steadfast to the right road. ... A man never caught up in dreams, just the normal way of doing things. My thoughts were that if I kept it so, then nothing bad could happen. I thought if I could always play it straight and never allow too much deviation — never too much — then I'd always land on my feet.

One morning in April, Brenda just stayed in bed. I asked her, "Aren't you getting up for work today?"

"Not today, Frank. Don't feel like working."

"I see. ... Might you then go to work tomorrow or the next day?"

"No, Frank. I don't think I'm going to work tomorrow, either. Maybe I'll never go back to that place. Maybe never."

Brenda and I had each worked at the prison for many years, and we'd gotten used to the jobs, gotten accustomed to *the place.* It seemed good for us. Our life was comfortable — very regular. I couldn't imagine either of us working anywhere else. It was a way of life then in many ways … yes, a real way of life, indeed.

"So, it's all quite different now without her — harder to appreciate anything, harder to fit in, Doctor. I don't really like it. And then there's *the tower* and the block riot that time."

"Tell me about the riot will you, Frank? What really happened during the riot? What happened that seemed to alter your life so radically? Do you remember?"

I sat across from Dr. Barron Franken, a well-known psychiatrist who understood people that worked in "pens." He was a respected specialist and I was ordered to see him one-on-one, twice a week.

"I do remember, Doctor. I think I keep most of it in my dreams, but once in a while a bit of it oozes out, like a little pus seeping out from some deep wound."

"Your record states that you were directly involved in some of the violence?"

"Yes, I was involved. … A man with some kind of weapon was on a rampage in G Block and I stopped him, on the Governor's orders. I never knew this man in prison, but he was in the sun and in my sights."

"Was someone killed during the riots — a guard or prisoner? Were they supposed to be shot during the outbreak?"

"I don't know if anyone wanted to be killed, Doctor, but the orders were given — and it's our job, always to follow and complete orders. And we do…yes, indeed, we do."

In his head, Frank hears, *"Do you want to take a walk with me, Frank? It's early…are you up yet? … Ready for the day? It's like spring here, Frank, like spring…and I feel so much better here, Frank…so much better.'*

"Sure, honey, let's take a long walk," he answers her silently. *"There's a park here or just down the road from here. … Let's hold hands and take a walk in the park, eh?"*

"I remember smiling smiles from deep inside. I was so happy to just be with her — so happy to just share some 'good time' with her then. … After that day, she seemed to disappear. … She seemed to be moving farther and farther away from me … never knew exactly why but it sure was happening. … Yes it was. … No way I could have denied it…no way."

***

He recalled again and again the targeting of the prisoner from the tower, the adjustment and the targeting of the man with his special rifle and sight. Using all the long hours training with that rifle and that advanced laser sight…so many hours.

"Could you pass me the milk, Frank? Can't eat oatmeal without milk, Frank. Need some good milk in my cereal, Frank…not much without it."

Frank automatically passed the milk jug to Brenda, who stopped suddenly and then poured the milk on her cereal.

"There's never really anyone to talk to me. … One assumes there is — a friend…a woman…a wife…someone — but few listeners are there. … Some are trained to listen, but generally no one really listens."

Brenda put a few blueberries on her cereal and then glanced over at Frank, listening with her eyes but continuing crunching on her cereal.

"I've been thinking of going away for ten days, Frank…to do some enhanced training. … Could you live with that right now, Frank?"

A few seconds roll by, but Frank remains silent, glaring at her every few minutes as he tries to delve into her closed little world.

"Frank, did you hear what I just said? I'd like to go to New York to do some advanced physical training for the company. … Can you live with that right now, Frank…or should I cancel and wait until the next training maybe?"

There is absolute silence in the room for a few seconds, and then Frank looked up at Brenda. … "Why don't you do what's necessary, Brenda? … It's not necessary to stay here for any particular reason"

Brenda continues shoveling down the cold wheat squares. The crunching makes a good deal of mouth noise as she continues chomping into the grains. "All right then, Frank. I'll make arrangements to take my trip at the end of the month…like nothing happened."

"Nothing did happen. And I don't need you here, Brenda. I've always been able to take care of myself, so why should it change now? … Why?"

"Well maybe because of the trauma at the prison last month and your direct part in it, Frank?"

"No, it didn't affect me, not one grain of it — no effect. No, you just head to New York and get some solid training in. … Maybe the separation will do us both some good … after—"

Brenda stared across at Frank and looked deep into his eyes, seeming completely unprepared for his words. "Frank, maybe the end of the month is too soon for me to leave. … I can stay if you want."

"No…don't stay. Take off. … Do your New York training and return fully brightened and refreshed. … Jolly and I will be fine."

"All you have to do is feed and water Jolly, Frank, nothing else. … I hope he'll be fine."

"As I said earlier, Brenda…go train and enjoy yourself. … You need a break from work, home and especially me. … It'll be a real good thing for you."

Brenda takes her empty bowl and deposits it in the sink, moves back to the table, then grabs Frank's nearly empty bowl. "Finished, Frank?"

"Oh yes…yes I'm finished with it. … It hit the spot for me for sure — maybe a banana could have helped — even so, it hit the spot for sure."

Frank just sits in front of the television staring into the tube blankly for the rest of the night — even after the networks sign off. Nothing seems to connect him with anything, every part of him appears utterly void — a man lost somewhere, where might be the best question. The telephone rings several times. It's Frank's brother Eddie.

"Hey, brother. ... How you doing? ... Putting it all back together yet?"

"You know, Eddie, I don't quite know what you're talking about. ... Piecing the 'book' together I guess. ... Lately it seems like most of life is a riddle. ... Maybe it'll all start making sense. ... Maybe all I need is a little work, you know?"

"Sure, brother, sure. ... I can easily understand how you must feel."

"You can? ... I doubt it, Eddie. ... Don't understand how many can understand how I feel after what I saw that day."

"Hey, you're a professional, Frank, hired by the 'state' to do what they order you to do. ... You *must* follow their orders and it's your job to protect the state...the whole state. ... Yes?"

Frank holds the telephone in his hand quite hard and stares blankly at the mini-receiver, not sure of what was said or what the answer should be...not sure at all.

"Yes, before I answer you, Eddie, I must think about it. ... Not so easy an answer. A lot goes into a response like this, Eddie...quite a lot!"

Frank moves slowly across the room with telephone receiver in hand, and stops in front of the television. He hesitates and pushes the top button on the receiver console.

"All right, Eddie, let me think about what you're saying and I'll just call you later. ... Right?"

"Right. ... You will call me later then? ... Tonight? ... Right? ... Promise?"

"Yes, I do promise to call you back, Eddie...sometime tonight. ... You need an explanation I guess...I guess..."

For about an hour Frank holds the receiver in his hand — his eyes fixed fully on the dead television screen — and presses the buttons activating nothing. Suddenly, the television clicks on and the volume blasts to extreme highs that continue unabated. ... Frank's face perspires and heavy beads of sweat appear on his chin and brow. His eyes bulge as if he's just exited the tenth inning in a world champion pitching battle.

The trigger, I can still feel the trigger, the way I lightly squeezed it. ... Never wanted it to jerk upward...never wanted the shell to reject. ... The simple forefinger against the metal, nothing to squeeze really — like pushing on a nipple...light pinch almost. ... Something calling me to depress the metal...some pressure on it. Can't remember the incident, not fully...all the noise, the chaos, people screaming. ... Shot going off...men stabbing other men...hostages in front of targets. ... Trained for all situations — all. We were constantly trained to work around any situation...our minds trained for response so perfectly united with the job.

Frank's eyes slowly close and a relaxed look falls over his face. ... The pressure abates, and somewhere he finds a place of peace in his exhausted and pinched soul. For moments, a refuge of silence.

Early the next morning Frank snaps awake as the telephone rings, his eyes half-open, dulled and half-awake, he answers, "Brenda? Guess I slept on the couch all night. I remember so little of what happened after Eddie called. Guess I was supposed to call him back."

"Did you? ... Did you call your brother back? ... Did you sleep through the call...or did you just forget?"

"No, I never called him back. ... When we were kids I always took care of Eddie. He never had to worry much about anything, 'cause big brother Frank was there...later in life it's much the same."

"So, why don't you get off the phone with me and call him back? ... I'll be home about noon...have to do some shopping first. ... Long shift tonight, Frank. ... Worried about you and worked too hard...truly a lot of hospital stuff happening last night."

Frank once again stares into the receiver, and continues to reflect on the earpiece. He waits patiently for some sound...standing with the receiver in hand, glaring at it.

"So, again, Frank, I'll be home about noon. Eat some cereal and fruit, and I'll see you then. ... Maybe we can talk before I sleep. ... All right?"

"Sure...sure. ... Yes, we'll have a talk, honey."

"All right. ... When I get there. ... Bye."

Frank automatically hangs the phone up as if he were unconnected from the call…from the task. He seems like he's in another place far from where he stands. … He walks, robot-like, over to the kitchen and grabs a bowl. He fills it with cereal and fruit…then adds some two percent milk.

I always wanted to help people when I was a kid, always acted out the ambulance driver when we played war or other games. … Always helped people…saved them from death or other great pain. Never thought of myself as a sniper. Never saw the use of snipers in war or especially in prison work…but there's always room for snipers. Maybe those are the kinds of jobs we will have for the future. … Why help when few really want you to help?… All they want is orders — orders to be followed blindly. … Follow my orders! … When I order it, you must do it — always follow orders!

A few seconds pass as Frank slowly spoons his cereal into his mouth. He pushes each bite in exactly, correctly, with military precision, feeding himself and following Brenda's orders. He listens as the telephone rings in the living room, yet he can't envision talking to anyone. He lets the telephone ring and ring again….

Frank pushes his chair back and moves quickly to the bathroom sink, lowers his head and washes his face in very cold water. *Sometimes cold water is the only thing that clears thought. … Did the same for me most of my life. … Why stop now?*

The telephone rings again. Frank carries a small cold towel with him and wipes his face as he moves into the living room to pick up the receiver.

"Hello? … Oh, hi, Eddie. … Didn't think you'd get back to me so quickly."

"Just finished watching a documentary on public television … *The Collective Two Hundred Years of The U.S. Marine Corps.* … Makes me proud. You must also feel that about our connection."

"Well, Eddie, haven't thought much about it lately…not much at all these days. Have a bunch of other stuff on my mind."

"Well, just going back to our earlier conversation, Frank, about responsibility. Well, you know that stuff really ties your nuts together. ... When you tie in all that really means...based on a Marine two-hundred year history of responsibility...gives you something to grab on to... something to live for, something 'yes' to believe in. .... Responsibility is what the Corps is about, Frank. ... Yes indeed, brother. ... Can't you see that? ... You know, as it relates to your job at the prison?"

Frank sits in a large sofa chair and glares at his sixty-inch television screen blankly with the sound muted. ... He sits and stares into a void with no emotions and listens automatically to his brother with the receiver pressed against his left ear.

"Yeah...there's a weird connection between the Marines and prison. ... But in general, I just don't see it. ... Never spent any time as an MP in the Marines. ... Maybe if I had...then maybe it would make sense — tradition of responsibility and all that. ... Maybe.

"Frank, maybe you should just take some time off. ... Yeah, just take a few days off. ... You need some rest. ... Just take yourself to a DVD store and rent some good film or another. ... There's a few good ones on The Corps. ... Might just make some real sense to you, eh?"

"No, Eddie...doubt that I'll be going down to the video store soon. ... Maybe I need a week off. That might be fine. ... And that film about The Corps...no, I won't be renting one of them. ... Not today or anytime."

"Well you just get some rest, read or watch a good television series ... hold hands with Brenda ... have a nice dinner somewhere home-like together...talk to her. ... All of that might 'lessen your burden' as Dad would say. ... Promise that you'll call me in a couple of days? Again, call me soon and tell me how you're doing. ... Get a little rest. ... All the best to Brenda...and just relax. ... I'll be waiting for your call. ... Bye."

Frank slowly puts the receiver down into its charging holder. ... He fumbles with it, having trouble getting it to fit. ... He keeps fumbling with it trying to get it to fit...finally watching he quickly gets it to fit and the charging light turns green.

He looks up at the clock, stands up and then slowly moves to the kitchen where he takes out a pitcher of cold water and drinks from it. He moves to the faucet and splashes cold water on his face with his right hand. He stares at the clock again, seemingly unable to get his eyes off it. He then automatically opens the refrigerator door, grabs some salami, mayo and some wheat bread and quickly puts a sandwich together. He takes a cold beer out and twists the cap off. ... He swallows two gulps and begins to stare at the digital kitchen clock again — viewing all in a kind of cold, unattached personal space.

The front door suddenly opens and Brenda walks in. She looks somewhat frazzled but immediately moves a few steps, turns the television off and calls Frank into the room. "Frank, can you come into the living room to speak to me? ... Need to talk. ... Been thinking about a few items for a while. ... Yes, I have...quite a while."

Frank looks up. His nose twitches slightly as if he'd just smelled something foul in the air ... a feeling of foreboding. ... His guts know something.

"Yeah, hold on a minute. Let me grab a chocolate bar and I'll be right in." *There's a tone in her voice ... something different. ... It's difficult to put a finger on it but something has changed.* He prepares his mind for whatever is coming.

Soft lights and subtle jazz play on the CD behind them. ... Soft and inconsequential yet professional music and singing by Michael McDonald — light but there.

"Music sounds good, doesn't it, Frank? Reminds me of some of our best times together. Yes?

"Do you remember Harry Swank's bar? He never had anyone but the best jazz piano people ... always the best musically. ... How many times did we sit there and listen to all those champs play? ... How many times?

"Many, maybe too many, Frank. That might be the place I learned to drink ... really drink — drink hard, drink deep and just stay sloshed."

"Sometimes it's good to be sloshed ... people need it at times. ... A little too much work kills much of what hurts ... but music, it just beats along in its separate rhythm somewhere in-between the hurt and the drink. … Sound, good sounds and drink can muffle and at the same time ease it all."

The music takes the two partners back to a time where they certainly learned to enjoy each other's company. Frank closes his eyes to go somewhere inside where he can enjoy his recall. The sun pokes the last of its golden rays through the dusty blinds as the only sounds left in the room are breathing, ice cubes clinking and silence — the music has stopped.

"Tell me, Frank, do you actually feel like we're the same two people that held hands so tightly at Harry's?"

"No, we've changed, gotten older. Maybe we've lived more of a life since then. … Lived on harder and less romantic ground I guess. … Happens to most couples…just got to balance it altogether somehow."

"We're different people now, Frank, interests not at all the same …and the roads taken are far different. There are many paths for us, Frank… not all the same."

"Don't see it all as so different after seventeen years, Brenda. Anyway, why would it be the same? … We all got to move forward in our own ways, don't we?"

"Have you ever thought that the 'we' in our marriage has shifted? … More like you and I kind of separate…kind of alone on far different journeys?"

"You know, Brenda, I never really think that way. … We've always been together in some way haven't we?"

"Maybe at one point, Frank, or maybe at more than one. … As for now, we're not together and haven't been for the last five years at least."

Frank sips his drink, listens as the ice clanks against itself and then against his teeth. … He seems suddenly to understand the new direction of the conversation.

"So, you laying the separate trails shit on me are you, Brenda? … Are you taking a new journey out with another…or just a skipping along on your own?"

"There is no other, Frank. I'm just plain tired, sour on what I am — what we've become — and see that we've left love on a trail somewhere behind us. ... I need love, Frank. ... I need a man who can love me — and I need to love him fully. ... I miss that, Frank."

"So, you're going? ... You've thought about it for a long time is the line...and you're just ready to go, eh? You're ready to be 'free' to have your own life...kind of without burdens? ... Burdens like me, eh?"

"The feelings are gone, Frank. Been gone for some time. ... Haven't you noticed anything different? ... So why continue? ... Don't know where all the feelings went...maybe it's old...maybe it's just time. ... It just doesn't fit anymore. I'd say that there's too much of what we had that's just dead for each of us. ... What is the point of marriage without *something*, Frank? ... Something—" Brenda shakes her drink and rattles the ice several times trying to dissolve them in the liquor...then she just stares at Frank's face over the top of her cocktail glass.

For a short period, there is just silence again except for the ice. ... Frank says nothing. ... Brenda realizes there is just something dead in him — something deep in his gut that somehow died right in front her.

"So, Brenda, what do you plan to do...after so many years together?"

"There's no one else in my life, Frank. Don't worry about that — not yet at least."

"Not easy for me to talk about this or much else. In fact...I'll just wander over for the bottle...and you can do whatever you want. Eh?"

Frank moves slowly and directly to Brenda and kisses her forehead. He then walks towards the kitchen and grabs the bourbon bottle. He pours some in his glass after he grabs some ice cubes from the freezer and then walks back to the living room across and over to his two Middle Eastern throw rugs. Brenda has left the room. There is utter silence. Frank automatically sits down and snaps the television remote on to the *CBS Evening News*. He then grabs the phone next to him and calls his brother.

"Hello, Eddie? Well yeah...actually Brenda's decided to leave. Take off, find her way on her own, etc."

"I see. ... Does she have somebody? ... Did she say anything about that?"

"No, Eddie, she has no one now, so crank those thoughts down. ... She's not screwing the paperboy. She's simply had it with 'us'. There is no 'us' anymore, it's just Brenda alone and Frank alone. ... That's all there is, Eddie...all of it."

"Sounds like Brenda's been leaving or thinking about it for some time, Frank. Doesn't sound like an instant decision...no, not at all."

"What does it matter, Eddie? She's on her way out and maybe she's completely right. ... Lately I don't respond with the mind of a husband, friend or lover — not much there anymore, Eddie. ... After seventeen years she's got a right."

"A marriage is a contract, Frank. Probably one of the most solid ones there is, from many perspectives. It's the most rock-like contract historically and culturally there is. ... It's not meant to be broken so easily."

"Society has changed, Eddie, changed in vast ways. It just doesn't operate the way you think it should, nothing operates like you think it should, Eddie...that's the past."

"Right, Frank, that's why our societies are crumbling, brother, deteriorating right in front of us on a daily basis ... worldwide and massive."

"Let's not go there, Eddie...not there. ... I'll call you sometime tomorrow. Bye."

Frank looks up at the ceiling as he hangs up, ending the conversation with Eddie. At the same time, tears stream from his eyes. He grabs a piece of paper and says, "Let me say it better..." and begins writing a note to his brother, Brenda, and all concerned others.

To Brenda, Eddie and to all who may be concerned:

I've lived through the Gulf War, lived and worked through prison and been on the street most of my life ... taken care of my younger brother Eddie. No family to speak of except each of you, and so this note must suffice as a fitting way of saying ...well let me say it far better.

Every day, massive and deep emotional feelings began to move into daily life as I continued drifting away from all who were close to me. Drinking for most times became my only brother, only friend, only wife. I could hear only chunks of ice in a crystal glass; all else seemed to fade into some kind of arbitrary fog.

During the Gulf War our Company was to lead the investigation into enemy killed, whether by direct hit or combat, and evaluate the weapons involved. We were the deep interpreters of the methodologies of death, whether through massive accurate weapons or release targeting.

Most of the actual groundwork was mundane other parts of it were dangerous, because of the special and classified use of depleted uranium. After fire and targeting, contamination remained inside and outside many of the destroyed Iraqi military vehicles and splayed body parts. Everywhere was extraordinary carnage, brutality and gore beyond what you'd see in any super-graphic DVD game.

Perhaps the disconnected nature of the killing made it easier for many of those targeting these Iraqi tanks, vehicles and troops. It was like an open attack electronic PlayStation of death resulting in far worse results than any in the history of combat.

Perhaps it was the absolutely split nature of destruction that became something like a newly released video game called "Killing in Mass." The Iraqi's were killed in large clusters, and many of the deaths were gruesome and painful. ... The depleted uranium and phosphorus shells driven down on them from above caused collateral deaths. Torn apart bodies were strewn everywhere. No one escaped this total sonic and chemical firebombing. It was definitely a hit test for the Navy and Air Force attack jets.

And so, the company made of various squads and platoons wandered like rats through the carnage of this undaunted killing assault on targets of war. Destroying both iron and flesh came via distant orders, somehow making assignments to massively kill by detachment. None of us could keep completely together. The weakest and the fiercest were one on this killing field — three weeks out in those death sands were enough. ...

Those inhuman killing plains of dust, blood and blowing poisoned sand mixed again and again with the depleted uranium and other chemical horrors causing more human sacrifice. ... The carnage was layered upon itself ... and it affected our minds most severely. These ghostly memories grind deeply into me. They sank even deeper into one or more of my platoon brothers.

In the end when we got stateside, they somehow by media proxy ended all history related to these horrific events and experiences. Forever wiped out with a stroke of "erasure media." Suicide notices were continuous after the Gulf War. Brothers, family and friends — men I knew, respected and loved —became "dust myths of history." Little was said about it, and less was reported about these veterans other than the usual local obituaries in local newspapers. Few, if any, think about the soldiers who survive. They are the "forgotten," pushed aside and in many cases lost — lost to themselves and lost to the world...additional victims of war.

I squeezed the trigger on an inmate named Michael Chavez last month, all done from the high tower above the prison. After that incident, many of the images from Iraq came back to haunt me. ... They returned and none of those images were easy to live with ... not at all. Few can really understand the pain of war unless they personally experienced it and wear its particular mark on their soul.

Since the end of the Gulf hostilities, I lived with no peace. For twenty years, no inner peace, only dreams and visions haunting my mind through many a sleepless night. With each dream, I saw a retreat from those I loved, and shooting Michael Chavez, squeezing a trigger from a distance, broke my connections with most everyone and everything.

I drank more from then on, and the relics of some piecemeal life were all I had. ... Same as other soldiers experienced. ... I had no one to talk to...most nearly all of my close friends were lost or dead by the mid or early two thousands. ... Yes, missing and lost, even if they were still breathing and walking.

The bullet I shot tore into Michael Chavez and I saw it enter his flesh, up close. ... He was just another "human target" — a target to be erased just as any target is. Finally, a connection was made between this man's life and my life in *'the game of life'* and that game wasn't worth playing anymore. ... That thought came to me quite hard and seemed directed right at me.

The drink is fine, and the night closes in on me as the candle I lit earlier tonight burns slowly out. And I, like the flickering candle and shadowed light, take my leave like some distinct words out of Hamlet. The ice in the crystal glass has no golden fluid to keep it company. Soon it will all just melt away into cold water and little else...

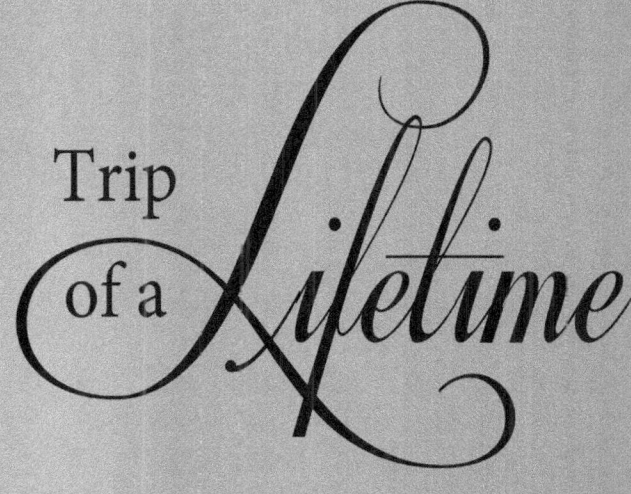

Trip of a *Lifetime*

Trip of a Lifetime

[That it was....]

The Miami Airport was extremely large, hard to manipulate, and logistically compromising. After eight arduous hours, we finally boarded the Continental Super-Jet 767 for Lima, Peru. There were three seats together separated by aisles, it was a plane nearly filled to its 300-person capacity. Peggy Lee and I sat there in the middle seats in the central section of the plane. We had a 15-hour compound flight to endure, and any long flight always meant 'semi-torture' to a seasoned traveler.

We were prepared with all the accouterments of extended night travel including the California night heroin — Ambien. Peggy Lee was a reluctant traveler, a woman who traveled little and didn't really have the understanding for extended excursions because of limited experience and training. During most of the trip she seemed somewhat scared, probably because she had never been out of the country...plus, being from North Carolina she was quite provincial in most things. I did what I could do to ease her anxiety.

"Do you think the Ambien will help me sleep? ... You know I really need to sleep, especially landing at such high elevations. Eleven thousand feet, right?"

"Yes, 11,000 feet. It's high but we're ready, in fact according to the guidebook if we chew a bit of coco leaves that may help us with extreme elevation."

"Right. … How in the world do you know it works? … Did you ever use it?"

"No, but I believe it works because the Peruvians have used it for centuries. They've been adjusting to heights of up to 22,000 feet or about 8,000 meters during their time living in the Andes. It's the second highest mountain range in the world."

"Well damn it, let's hope you're right and they know what they're doing, or this trip could get each of us as sick as an old tick-ridden hound dog."

I looked at Peggy Lee directly and said nothing, just opened my book for a couple of hours as she grabbed her large earphones and watched a chase movie, paying little to no attention to me. I reviewed some of the places we'd be traveling … the central places and some of the smaller side trips that would be more interesting. Of course, I was especially excited about walking the paths of Machu Picchu.

A
Lover's Prophecy

A Lover's Prophecy

A friend of mine called that morning. We'd once shared a seminar with at the local community college. … We co-lectured on civil disobedience and sometimes she and I accompanied each other to appropriate places around the city. In fact, Sarah and I during that year would often attend various ballets. … Coming up was a special performance scheduled for the college by the Colorado State University Dance Company. I didn't have to think about it very long when Sarah invited me to the performance. I loved modern ballet and had enjoyed it all my life … I quite easily committed to accompany her to the performance.

After hanging up the phone, I thought about it because I had plans with other friends to have dinner, dance some, maybe chase a few women, etc., yet something deep inside me said, 'Go with Sarah'…so I listened to my gut.

I headed to my office and started working on some mid-term papers I needed to read, critique and grade…yet I kept thinking about the Colorado State Dance Company arriving at the college's perfect performance hall. It was a wonderful venue for dance, music and symphony.

After finishing the majority of the papers, I soon jumped into the shower and cleaned up. After getting dressed and grabbing half a banana, I called my friend Tom Lopez to see if he'd meet me for dinner and a drink. I talked him into going out, as he was in for a quiet evening when

I first called. He was into my plan when I mentioned Antonio's, a place he truly enjoyed.

So, I hopped in the car and drove downtown and met Tom at Antonio's. We had visited the restaurant many times, usually to enjoy the food and a sharp political discussion. Getting into the evening, Tom danced with a black-haired beauty to a modern Flamenco fusion guitar. ... Each of us truly enjoyed the night — we spent three hours together.

I mentioned the Colorado State Dance Company and Tom seemed quite surprised at my enthusiasm regarding dance, in particular this one.

"Hey, maybe it's the magic of this guitarist, by the way one of the best I've heard here. ... The music stimulates my imagination and digs into some raw part of me."

"And you've only had two drinks, amigo. Can you imagine what three would do? *Quizás?*"

Tom hit the nail on the head ... something quite different was turning me on. ... Where it came from and what stimulated it, I could not say for sure...yet something was certainly there, stirring deeply inside my guts.

I kept working through many hours over the next three days and no matter what I did I seemed to demand more — more of me, more of my students. My overall energy was burning in all areas of endeavor from teaching to my constant mountain bike workouts — all was at a new and demanding pace. I also kept thinking about the upcoming ballet and Sarah, never before had I looked so forward to a semi-professional ballet.

One Friday before the night of the ballet Thomas and I rode 30 miles to Little Butte Peak, it's normally a grueling uphill battle...resistance against the best of 'wills.' Miraculously, Thomas and I raced each other and other riders through the second crest where we had to stop, rest, eat and turn around. Usually we 'ditched' the pace at level one of the peak, yet this time each of us seemed to demand that we 'go' just a little further.

We slowed the pace on the return ride, and we stopped at the 'F' Street Café in Moffet, where we enjoyed a local beer and a great sandwich…always a wonderful treat. Thomas and I talked about our fine ride and the young Red-tailed hawk we saw. … The day seemed to bring me more and more internal power — I felt like an inflatable health doll getting better and better with each passing hour of the day.

"Nice ride old friend…kind of tough!"

"Oh, I don't know, Thomas, we've done it before. It just seemed to all come together on that ride today. … Yes!"

"Hey, still looking forward to seeing Sarah and going to the ballet?"

"Well it's not a date really, she and I have engaged each other for many years — years we've enjoyed being together. It's kind of good being with a woman — one you actually like — at an event, and it's just that… no romance, no sex, just some solid companionship. …. I love that — it frees me."

"Does it do the same for Sarah or is that just the way you feel?"

"You know, to me she is just as free as that hawk today. … We seem to have a perfect understanding of who we are…and who we are together."

"Sounds good, wish I had a Sarah to accompany me at times. … Me? All I get is Hilda, Tia and Marene…all we share is fatty foods and long rough unloving bouts at best. … It's more like high-jumping than romance…companionship may be a far better release."

Thomas and I separated from each other at midtown, he rode to the south of town and I rode to the north. … He stayed in a guesthouse behind another home owned by his mother and sister. He'd never been too far from his family in all the years we'd been riding — in all the years we'd been friends.

I slept late the next morning, guess the ride had taken more out of me than I realized — a good sleep always heals. Got up and cooked up a fine veggie omelet with a side of smoked chicken cheddar sausage and local artisan bread — wonderful morning starters.

That afternoon I read and graded Critical English papers…some were excellent. The rest of the day was television and tennis, the *Australian Open* was on and it always excited me. Every year those athletes seemed to get better…so much professional grace and personal drive.

After that, a good shower and the 'good stuff' were needed to prepare for a fine ballet to come. … I danced occasionally and casually, with emphasis on dressing in some of the sharpest clothes I owned. … It just felt good!

After a short cell phone call to her, Sarah picked me up at seven that evening in front of the apartment house. We drove to the college's student recital hall — a new college foundation building, one of the best acoustically designed buildings on any Colorado campus. We climbed our way to the second balcony after having a glass of red wine each in the lobby. Sarah always managed to get the best and most practical seats in the house…I was always wowed by her practical capabilities.

We made our way past several sitting folks until we found our numbered seats smack in the center aisle. We talked briefly about another performance we had seen and enjoyed. Somehow we'd never realized that we both enjoyed any ballet by Sergey Prokofiev, which once again we would experience on this particular night. For each of us, Prokofiev's music — particularly the children's works — always resounded in magnificent aural colors and 'frames of sound' that continually excited the audience.

Within five minutes, the stage turned quite black and for several seconds it remained so. Then an intense single light appeared center stage followed by a single female dancer in a tight body 'glove' who seemed to appear from nowhere. The dancer joyously opened many visual molecules of light spinning and weaving in magical movements that 'entangled' the mind.

I tapped Sarah on the shoulder to see if I could use her small stage binoculars, something I'd never done before at any stage performance we'd shared. I was both enamored and dazzled by this twisting body on the stage in front of us.

I viewed her enchanted movements for five glorious minutes, hypnotized by the spell she cast. … Her presence on the stage, her pure power and the perfection of the dance movements absolutely enthralled me. This was a special and unexpected performance.

For these five or so *lost minutes* I was in another world — never before had I experienced a dancer with such raw and yet professional power. Once, in Barcelona, I had experienced another dancer, singer and gypsy guitar player who managed to lock and captivate my mind in a similar way…lost was I in the dance, the dancer and the coordinated ethnic clapping and chanting. It was 21 years ago, but in my mind I could still see the dance and hear the music, tap dancing and guttural voices singing to the rhythms of short Rodrigo pieces.

I was completely lost and spellbound by that collection of sounds and dance and ethnic heart connections…rhythms beating again and again through my common brain…and here I was again with a single ballet dancer creating almost the same experience for me on this local performance stage. There are many avenues of entertainment mixed with love, and here again 21 years later, I confronted yet another…unbound connected tissues chasing the emotional and erratic underpinnings of the glue in my soul.

I reveled internally, watching and understanding what the dancer was sending to me and the rest of her audience. … She was a rare beauty — 'an exotic love' — and it was a performance beyond any I'd experienced — ever.

Sarah tapped me on the wrist. She wanted to use the stage glasses. I snapped out of my trance and handed them to her silently…. I continued to follow the dance and the dancer with my naked eyes until five other dancers joined her on the stage to finish the first segment of the ballet.

A short intermission followed and Sarah and I made our way to the upper balcony lobby for another glass of Cabernet. We 'small talked' about the performance and I listened both to her and the others around me as they verbalized opinions on the first segment of the ballet and the single female ballerina — some interesting comments. … I quickly reflected through the night's program guide to find the name of the main dancer ... Hannah Soldez. Ah, Hannah Soldez, my mind was disquieted and at the same time electrified...

Once again, we were in our seats viewing the production from our nearly perfect center viewpoint. Four striking athletes — muscular male dancers — performed in a spider web of coordinated and ultra-synchronized moves. ... Their costumes were jet-black with small sections of their neck areas exposed, revealing nakedness — quite subtle and innocent.

After several minutes of the dancers weaving like black and white puffer fish moving in handcrafted choreographed brilliance, Hannah Soldez entered center stage from behind another dancer. ... She swiftly joined the fast-moving weaving patterns turning in and out, in and out in opposite direction of the male dancers.

My eyes began to spin as I followed the continuous interweaving patterns moving at advancing speeds. My head itself began to spin as 'they' moved in the other direction. ... It seemed as if my eyes couldn't take the information in fast enough. ... Everything inside my brain seemed to change...like some deeper cellular structure altering and my inner body automatically responding. It was as if my sweeping mind took me to some mystic stage beyond my body with no interference or natural protection from any other bodily system — there was no control at all, none at all.

Finally, Hannah led the dancers in wider patterns, twisting in a multi-cornucopia of patterns and forms sewn exquisitely upon the stage. They circled wider and wider until all the male dancers exited stage right...the rhythms and patterns of dance and music perfectly synchronized.

Again, at the end of the performance, Hannah was the single figure remaining in a lighted circle on center stage. Her arms slowly reached toward the sky, her breathing exhausted yet she stretched her arms higher and higher and her body began to spin like a top or twirling dervish dancer. ... The spectacle was her — her turning, her frame, her very grace, and her exposed soul.

I was caught like a fly in the web she wove with her body. ... I was seeing the divine spirit of 'love' moving in *perfect content* before me. ... Who was this Hannah Soldez?

Once again, all the lights dimmed to black and the stage was raked and empty. My heart was racing again as I got up caught in it — in it all. ... Then my breathing slowed as the second intermission bell rang twice.

Sarah tapped me on the shoulder, waking me from the trap I'd fallen into…as if I were coming out of a deep trance.

"Where were you?"

"Somewhere else for sure. ... Yes, someplace different no doubt."

"Let's get more wine and talk some. Okay, Michael?"

"Yes, yes let's walk down there. I need to walk for sure…need to run maybe — that might be too hard in this crowd though."

They each laughed as they moved down the stairs toward the second balcony and the wine bar.

"What a performance that second act was — most intriguing. I was definitely caught up in it."

"Yes, Sarah…you got caught in it like I was…tied up for sure and totally mesmerized by Ms. Soldez and her projected grace. ... Never felt anything like it — ever."

"Felt? Michael, am I hearing you correctly? I can't ever remember you using that word after any dance or any performance we've ever attended together!"

"Well I certainly did 'feel' this one. Was drawn into it like an insect to a silk web. ... Yes *feeling* more than I could ever imagine.

"There was a kind of smooth starkness in it that seemed to pull one directly in—

"I was *so* pulled in. ... And the professionalism…almost flawless — actually crowning in every aspect they unmasked on the stage. ... Quite a show!"

After our talk about the excellence of the performance, we once again climbed up the narrow stairs to our third level balcony seats.

Each of us was exuberant about this dynamic dance exhibition we'd just experienced.

Then it all began once again — the drums and undulating beats, the dancers interweaving between each other's bodies, the lights flashing in flawless rhythmic beaming interface. Hannah moved once again across center stage at a quickened pace, like a shooting star across a blackened sky. Stepping and darting in and out, she sprang like a panther, her boundless energy seemed to defy gravity — she was the space and the face was Hannah's.

The music built up and expanded in every direction like Stravinsky's "The Rites of Spring," and yet the pace and the tenor of the composition by Phillip Glass was radically different. The 'sounds' penetrated deep into our ears, and the pulsating cracks of noise and space punctuated the stage as Hannah and her troupe of dancers poured themselves into the performance, sweeping jumps to odd musical sounds both human and beyond human. The audience seemed petrified...held in a studied embrace until the very last section of this glorious performance.

The composer seemed to take the dancers back to the first act and yet he refused to let it go so easily. ... Somehow the dancers themselves weaved a story of birth and death all mixed to a crashing percussion crescendo sounding like collisions in the universe itself — openings and re-birth.

As it ended, the dancers lay head to head in circles around the stage — circles shaped in counter-clock directions. Then there was no sound as each dancer rose and crossed another circle disappearing in the blackened darkness of center stage. Each body moved into the darkness, one after the other after the other and Hannah was the last to move. ... One could almost feel her muscular angst, even from the upper balcony.

In the end, the stage was empty and completely black and all sound dead — giving way to absolute silence. Then applause and whistles like no other performance I'd ever attended topped with yells and heady screams of "Bravo!" After three or four curtain calls, the crowd started breaking up and leaving the theatre.

Then Sarah turned her head toward me and said, "What an exciting performance! Don't think I've ever experienced a dance performance at this level — ever!"

"Amateur!" I joked. "No, not amateur at all. I have to call it 'structurally professional' — that might be a more precise definition.

"You know, Sarah, through all the years that you and I have attended and witnessed many fine performances in the world of modern dance, and yet for a woman, maybe more for a woman, this was near perfection."

"For a woman? … Well I'm not sure I grasp the whole aspect of that statement —not really at all."

"For me, I saw an unconscious feminine level here that spoke, I believe, to some deeper part of a woman's core. … It's hard to explain it."

We continued down the last set of stairs in the new performance center and Sarah asked me if I'd like to meet the artistic director and the lead dancers in their dressing room. At first, I was surprised at the offer — it seemed to come out of nowhere. Yet I knew something new was coming with Sarah reporting in the arts section of the local newspaper.

"All right, Sarah. Guess I'd enjoy that. … Yes, I'd actually like to meet some of the key dancers."

In my mind I thought about talking to Hannah Soldez, the central and featured dancer. … *Yes, I'd love to meet her!* My thoughts must have apparent to Sarah as we pushed the door behind the staircase to enter the hall leading to the main women's dressing rooms.

We went into the large and quite warm dressing room. When I locked in the back corner to the side, there was Hannah still in her black costume, talking to a colleague. By pushing Sarah in the right direction, we carved our way through the crowd toward Hannah. As we approached, another reporter grabbed Sarah by the arm and started chatting with her about a recent local news story, so I approached Hannah separately.

I tried passing the two people in front of me, but one headed right toward Hannah and started talking. … Hannah now had a red scarf wrapped around her exquisite neck … the woman was then sidetracked before she could utter another word.

Hannah was enchanting, from her perfect size to her next to perfect dancer's shape and her muscular body balance only added to her powerful overall presence. She was the absolute image of an uncluttered woman — truly a "living soul" on her own. I stood directly in front of her for several seconds without uttering a word. I watched her green eyes dive to the depths of my soul as if she could dance on my very blood cells. For another few seconds, I lost contact with my "inner self," as if I were a Dervish Dancer lost in the mystic spinning corruption of personal entrancement.

"Hello, Hannah...you were most wonderful tonight. ... Yes, I sat in the balcony with Sarah and was mesmerized by your performance, and of course the troupe of dancers supporting you."

"Sarah did say she would be bringing her close friend Michael to the show, so I have some idea who you are."

Her words powered by those deep green eyes completely threw me off...it was as if I was running naked, holding a rugby ball waiting to be "hard hit" for blind possession. I consciously felt alchemy between us, a blend of which I had never confronted — ever — prior to this evening.

"Hannah, the last dance sequence — or the final crescendo of dance and music —were beyond words. ... The rhythms beat at my core, through my very essence—"

"Yes, it was meant to. That is exactly what we hoped to achieve both with our collective troupe and for our core audience."

Her voice had a soft and yet penetrating inner sadness. ... It was as if her voice was another dancer springing words and sounds on me.

"Tell me, Michael, did the last five minutes of the show absorb you... and I mean 'uniquely' absorb you as if nothing else mattered?"

"Yes. I don't know exactly why but there was such a combining totality of passions in the last moments of that performance in particular... wonderful!"

"It was designed and choreographed that way. It was all in our collective pre-plan and all of us moved and thought quite hard about it to pull it off. … You saw extraordinary passion flowing into your eyes and souls during the last sequence in particular."

I stood there in blinding awe, as if no one else was there in the world with us. … It was a very slow-motion synapse in a large cinema graphic — a period piece production. Then suddenly, as if we were in freeze frame, other mouths began talking around us, distorted and unfiltered sounds at first then becoming clearer — fan words spoken to Hannah.

"Give me your card, Michael, one with all your personal and business numbers. We will talk again soon?"

"Yes, here it is. … Your words charm me nearly as much as your dancing. … Here's the card. … Call me anytime…at any time and we can discuss more."

She smiled at me, grabbed the card and gently took my hands in hers before moving graciously to another person waiting to talk to her. She left me with a final quirky stare projected from her mysterious pool-like green eyes.

Sarah and I, soon after the meeting with Hannah, left the theater and she drove me straight home. We talked some about the tremendous dance performance we'd both experienced as we drove.

After a quick and relaxing shower, I climbed into bed and began re-reading *The Idiot* by Fyodor Dostoyevsky — one of my favorite all-time Russian pieces of literature. As I was about to close my eyes before dozing off, my cell phone rang. I read the number and didn't recognize it, yet answered automatically.

"Yes? … Yes I do. … I'm so glad you called me…and so soon." My mind started swirling off in rapid images."

"We know what transpired in the main dressing room after the performance, and each of us knew about the meeting way before 'the meeting' so the call should not be a surprise…at all."

I sat up in my bed and listened to her words carefully…somehow the raw energy of Hannah's potential stirred my very active mind.

"Can we meet again face to face? … Maybe a long lunch before you leave the area?"

"Of course, for a start…but I shall never leave —never ever. Do you know that?"

I thought about Hannah and her words again quickly for many silent moments. … I thoroughly knew we were somehow tied at levels I couldn't understand.

"Yes…I do know that. … I do understand…and I shall *meet* you… indeed!"

THE CAMP

The Camp

My memory was empty when it came to details of my capture, all insight related to it was very stale…

I could see glimpses of it. It was like seeing a mist in a vast dream…a mist over a greyish hole trying to form something…

Headed to Seattle from Portland, on the last Amtrak train, it was a dark night and I was quite tired — almost sleeping. Few passengers on the train, very few travelers …yes. I was sitting reading a newsletter. Sitting next to me across the aisle was a young woman with dark brown hair — she had a sweet smell.

Suddenly, four very large, masked men grabbed me, and asked my name. "Robert Fuller," I replied, then they proceeded to pull me off the train after demanding and executing an emergency stop. One of them, in fact the only one who talked, soon injected me with an electronic hypodermic as I walked slowly forward. I could not speak. It all happened quite fast and the next conscious thing I remember was that I awoke in the camp.

We've all had similar experiences; these were the words of many arriving in "The Camp." … The inmates in the camp repeated these words again and again like they *were taught* in the same way to each person who muttered them.

"The Camp" was outside in a very stark setting with boulders and huge rocks everywhere...in a dark scape. ... In all directions one could look there were no trees or shrubs...mostly grays in the horizon mixed in dry sand tones. Every part of the camp was set in 20-person individual compounds cut neatly in the ground, almost looking like a modern New Mexico pueblo scene more than anything else.

There was the men's compound and the women's compound, and there was absolutely no contact and no mixing of genders. This was strictly "forbidden" by Camp Rule #48. There were many rules and they were openly shown to us on dark blue digital displays — they were everywhere. ... For several nights I could see these blue displays when I slept, until I finally got used to them, then dream images finally ended.

So, in modern language I believe I've been *renditioned* here for around two years. No charge has ever been cited or ever issued directly to me. ... When I try to ask "the authority," they'd simply dismiss me with these same words, *"Your name will be coming up soon."*

Occasionally I see a bird or two entering the camp from the south — only birds are allowed in and out. Even that depends on their corridor within — the invisible force that binds-up the parameter fifty meters above the camp and on all sides. It is certainly restrictive.

There is no way out — absolutely no way. Even thinking about "out" is forbidden. Somehow that kind of thinking is displayed on the digital badge all of us wear. If "bad thoughts" are recognized, it can cause personal pain. If the yellow digital signal is lit up, Camp Rule #210 is invoked.

We are allowed 250 words a day. If that is exceeded, some quite harsh neck vibrations start as any "over-word" is uttered. One can never exceed more than three blasts because of the level of pain. The pain seems to be both a conscious and sub-conscious thing. It is deep pain, maybe intolerable pain — something beyond all else. ... This is Camp Rule 78 — 250 words.

"I managed to make a couple of friends at the compound during work times. One was Talago Wilson, an African-American in his mid-

60s…a wonderful human being. Then there was his good friend, Jake Cullen, an old circus roust-about from my old state of Georgia. Camp Rule 78 does cause an efficiency of language. It's especially difficult when you have friends, yet this efficiency is a hard rule and must be followed in all areas of The Camp.

"Did they share the compound with you? … Were they actually a part of your compound?"

"Yes, yes, they were part of the 20 inmates. All of course lived in four-person groups in separate adobe structures. … Separation always seemed to be a main element for those in The Camp —a major part of its core structure."

"Go on, please. … By the way, did you ever discover what it was or what you did that allowed them to intern you in The Camp?"

"No, I can't remember much, not much of it is clear now. … I just don't remember much about the capture, not much at all. … Yet I do recall something about a question — 'What are you detaining me for and what are you charging me with?'"

"Ah yes, many times there is no charge, no indictment and no trial… these days it all moves *quicker* to keep costs down. These places or secondary places seem more important to authorities, especially these days, according to my research. … *Now,* they have to prove the 'worth' of the captive to achieve their bonuses or precise goals. … Sometimes, they are referred to as tiered goals — it's all some kind of structural incentive system or technocratic terminology play."

"For many years I would be moved from place to place within "The Camp." I was not strictly positioned at one campground or another. I was moved every month, sometimes sooner. One thing that always bothered me was the kinds of sounds within the compounds. Sounds yes. … They depended on some sort of small manufacturing technology or work task actually performed at that particular compound. The sounds usually continued for sixteen hours a day, two shifts and then sleep for all!"

"What kinds of sounds are you talking about? … Give me an example … Can you describe it?"

"Well, at one compound at the southernmost part of the camp were the special bullet manufacturing units were, we molded shells using small presses and forges to create them…a real skill, almost an ancient art form. Those compounds were very popular according to Talago, my African friend. They gave the 'imprisoned' a distorted idea of a 'place of power, because of the fine grinding, forging and metal handling. … It was an interactive place to grow…it put 'man' into a man. … It was like a muscle, it was *like* a hunter-brain connected thing, he said. … So these compounds were very much in demand."

"When they captured you, did they *patch* you immediately? … Do you recall any patch being put anywhere on your body? Did you feel or see anything unusual?"

"You know it all happened so fast — during the brief rendition I was blindfolded and taken to The Camp. … I didn't feel or see much except their powerful arms and wrists, so super strong even for a relatively strong man — it was too much indeed. Yet remembering my first shower in Camp X-1, I did see a patch on my left inner thigh, but I could remember nothing. I could never connect with where I got the little patch, and no one ever put anything on me…yet somehow there remained a slight indentation on my right inner thigh."

"So, ah then, you do understand that probably everything you did or will do in the future will be *tracked, watched or listened to?* You shall continue to be followed, most likely for the rest of your natural life!"

"When it all took place, and it took place very fast, a patch or electronic surveillance device was the least of my worries. … All I wanted to do was get out! …I kept wondering what I had done…who put me into The Camp?

I had seen and talked to the journalist for several days, and wasn't sure why I was allowed to speak so freely to him, yet this "explanation" of my time in and before The Camp was important, so very important for me. In fact, one of the other compounds I worked at was very different — we made highly refined mobiles to hang above wealthy infants' cribs.

All of these were created in our design centers. ... Actually, I heard there were three compounds within The Camp that used high tech digital design machines and designers plus drafts-people who were trained while in The Camp or had previously developed outside skills that "the guardians" could use. [I never mentioned any of this to the journalist.]

Anyway, we made all the mobiles, but they had to be perfect and we used high grain cotton materials. Yes, both pure and very high grade. We worked with special tight-fitting plastic glasses on and every stitch on the little horse figures for the mobiles had to be excellent. Any that were imperfect, we rejected. "The Guardians" received bonuses for the most accurate work and were paid in fine silver coins. ... Jake Cullen told me this, yet my eyes never saw any exchange.

I remained at the mobile compound for several months. In fact, I was kept there for almost a year before I was told to move. Sometime after, my thoughts roved and dreamed through the night.

The journalist returned the next day to my small second story flat with more questions. "Did you ever try to escape from The Camp or any of the compounds?"

"No, there was no escape. Running away was not something that could happen. Breakout was a 'programmed impossibility'...a solidly programmed nix."

"Can you discuss the protections against flight?"

"Not really, but I can say this much...we were given training on computer screens and one of the programs involved 'flight.'"

"What did it depict? ... What was the visual like? ... Can you describe it?"

"There were posts and some visible electronic walls. ... They had no sound, as such, but they were striking and had multiple backup systems in case power or something failed. ... If a person tried to run through them he would be destroyed instantly. ... Once again this was designed to completely 'remove' any thought of escape. Suicide was the only path to freedom we all shared. To run through the posts meant one died immediately — charred body with little left of you."

"And you never tested them? Not even with a rock? ... You saw nothing except the visuals...and the narrative. Was there a purely written explanation of 'confinement'?"

"Yes, it was all explained very clearly, nothing could be more exact. In fact, at the far north end of The Camp I saw some posts that stretched out about 200 meters, and then I saw another. ... We were all silent about the posts — like they were mirages. ... All we could do was wait for any runners."

"Have you ever seen a runner try to bolt through the posts?"

"No, but my friend Jake Cullen did see one. He assured me that the visual shown in training was horribly accurate. ... No departure was possible...no, none at all."

"And beyond what I've already told you, there were some guardians in vehicles beyond the camp, watching all. There were patrols, mini-drones, voice detecting architecture, and small satellites making sure that no objects, bird or anything else could leave The Camp between the metered posts. ... Nothing, period."

"Yes, a tightly controlled system I would say. ... Yes, indeed...quite tight!"

⟨2⟩

In an enclave at the most remote northern end of The Camp, Robert works at assembling and steam forging cellular bandages for imprinting permanent identification. These are devices attached to the skin for 24 hours and then removed. At twenty-four hours, they become cellular and molecular and transition into a permanent part of a person's RNA and DNA.

James Scott once again is back interviewing Robert Fuller in his small city apartment in the central northeast section of downtown Seattle, Washington. "What did you actually assemble at Sub-Camp Enclave 7 in The Camp?"

Robert silently watched the journalist for several seconds, studying his eyes as he spoke. He watched his eyes move and sees his mouth move yet he doesn't fully understand the words exiting his lips. It seemed to him like an early childhood example of recognition, a silent yet slow recovery, a mental retrenchment …like going nowhere to somewhere… or where someone should be in a "normal conversation."

Finally, he answers, "Well at Enclave 7 we assembled and constructed very finely designed electronic ID badges that were used in our camp and several others in the U.S. and around the world."

"From what I understand, these badges were put on the skin and identified the prisoner forever…in perpetuity. Am I right?"

"Yes, once the electronic imprint was 'melded' within the mix of skin cells and the RNA and DNA, this 'mark' would remain until the energy of life itself maxed out."

"Sounds like these were extremely sophisticated devices to be made and assembled in isolated special camps like you were in."

"Yes and no. … The higher technical elements were part sub-particle chips designed and built somewhere else…Bhutan I believe. Then these parts were tested and shipped to us at isolated camps…or at least this one."

"Are these built and assembled only here or do you actually know?"

"I don't know, but we had to be trained for weeks to be able to assemble them accurately. … Yes, coached for many weeks — ten hours a day, six days a week training and retraining."

"Were the men and women paid properly for their hours and fine work? If they were paid, what was the currency or deliverable?"

Robert turned his head and looked through a large picture window in his apartment that looked out into a large grove of trees that often had branches covered by crows — a bird that Robert enjoyed watching in silence. He usually watched them with his binoculars.

Coming back to the present, he said, "So, you asked if the workers in the camp enclaves…in particular #7 were paid. Right?"

"Yes, I asked you that before you looked out the window."

"Yes, they paid us on occasion, usually every two weeks. Yes, we were paid with a few silver coins, and we were told they were one hundred percent 'real' silver — worth far more than any paper currency."

"Did any of you ever test or check the value of the silver coins?"

"One of the workers was an x-coin master plus an expert in metals, he assured us that our coins were silver and worth 'our hours worked.' ... Not much was questioned beyond that...not much."

"Let's move to another subject, eh? So, when you knew you were to leave The Camp, how did you actually *feel* about leaving?"

"Don't know about feelings. ... I'd been at this camp for about 48 months and eleven days — that's a long time spent...a long time with no acknowledged offense."

"It was just recently that *some* of the limited information surfaced regarding these isolation camps...so most anyone who was involved is a story."

"Yes, a story. All of you seemed to be looking for a story — a story to read, a story to grab, or a story to listen to...one to imagine. ... A story then, *always* a story."

"What else do humans really have, Robert? Stories take us from one generation to the next...one culture to the next...always to the next. When the story ends we end. ... Don't you see that, Robert?"

"No, not really. ... But for several in this Camp whom I knew...yes, it is story and conversation that works...words for life...words for dreaming. ... That's what we wanted...that's just what we knew. ... Perhaps the only thing we knew."

"So, can you give me more details regarding The Camp? ... What else can you describe about your 48 months there?"

⟨3⟩

Robert sits at a long steel table with two other men. Again, his two closest companions have been ordered to work with him, having recently arrived from the outer enclaves of The Camp. They eat their automated meals, which are served from small glass delivery centers set up within the inside walls surrounding them — something resembling a New York automatized meal serving center. Talago Wilson and Jake Cullen sit beside and across from their friend Robert. It's exceptionally silent except for the sound of chewing, and all the eating process is done with semi-hardened cardboard utensils. Not much ambient sound either; most of the prisoners stay silent as they "take in" their food. It's almost another ritual for all at The Camp. ... Every activity at the camp seems to become ritual, rules become ritual for the long-term incarcerated.

"Robert, do you remember being in the clay centers with Boo and me?"

"Yes…seems like a long time ago now. ... Talago did mention that they were closing the clay centers one by one in every part of the camp. .. Is it true?"

"One has been removed from what I've heard, but there's still two open in the northern part of The Camp."

There's silence between the two men as they slowly continue eating the rest of their food. Talago keeps verbally pressing his enjoyment for the work at the clay centers.

"I'd like to rework some of my time back at the clay centers. . . One could say that if one must work, he might as well develop that potting skill. ... After a while it begins to flow through you like some artistic painting…or some other arty craft."

"Yeah, Robert, I kind a felt the same way. Maybe if Talago goes back or asks for a transfer, I just might join him."

"Well maybe the three of us should try to get back there together… work together again. ... Might just be a fine, fine idea…working together again."

"How'd ya think we can work it, boys?"

"I have one manager who seems like a possibility. ... Let me talk to Alberto. ... He might allow the three of us back, based on our old production records. … Maybe he'll score a bonus over it, eh? Anyway, they're always motivated by production. … May take a little time though."

"We all know one thing…we all have a little time."

After a group laugh, Talago grabbed his metal dish and took it to the washing basin and scrubbing system. Robert stood and went to wash his plate quickly, then put it into a large dishwasher. The other two men followed him, mimicking his actions.

⟨4⟩

Clay Center II

"My mind was fully occupied by the task, the creative work, the molding of the clay. … It was all of it — all other elements of life seemed to be somewhere else, somewhere in another dream place or reality. The clay center, the biggest of the northern ones, was clean — nothing was messy, it was *the sage* of incarcerated efficiency… a perfect mastery.

All the work, like all the work at The Camp, had to be done in absolute silence. All one could hear were the occasional sounds of breezes between the quiet workings of the foot driven potting wheels. One could also hear the quiet rustle of all the desert trees and shrubs surrounding the northern Camp post. Occasionally, I'd pause and stop working to examine a pot closely…then I would look outside for a few seconds, and listening and watching the winds blowing dust while I remembered parts of another life 'overspent' before The Camp."

"Other thoughts?"

"All of us found life in the clay center far better…it had a natural pace and rhythm. It was a 'heart' in itself. … It was an evolution of sorts… yes, it highlighted 'progress,' especially after an object was *finished* and glazed. Of all the tasks and work performed in the years at The Camp, the clay centers were somehow *more*. Yes *more*, satisfactory, something done, an accomplishment that was finished and then sold.

"The managers we had were 'easy' on the 20 clay inmates they man-aged. Not much was ever said, never a pat on the back for hard work or quality, productivity or skill...yet each craftsman knew. ... Yes, all knew how much growth there was just with a little guidance...only a little guidance."

"Go on, please?"

"At dinner, the second meal, I met Bob and Talago for another chat... allowed at the clay centers as a reward for 'good work.' Our 'allowed time' to chat was once a week for 30 minutes and was granted only to those who produced. Even then, it was only production approved by 'manage-ment.' Some of the discussions, in fact many of them, went beyond work and the clay objects or their sales, beyond our view. ... They were lofty discussions about the state of human affairs within the overall system ... and beyond The Camps.

"It's not all that simple or the same in the various camps spread around the country...at least according to sources I have talked to dur-ing these years. When the development objectives of The Camps are well met and are most successful, nothing 'bad' appears to happen. Yet, that is not so true of all Camps or 'craft sections' within Camps that didn't meet their financial goals. When we talked of this, Talago looked toward me in disbelief and quickly found himself redirecting the conversation to alternatives."

"So, Robert, when a Camp or craft group within a Camp is not suc-cessful, it all turns to something else?"

"Yes, my friend, and there is a terrible problem...there are no laws or governance regarding commercial activities by the owners. They are not officially sanctioned with regulations, because officially we are not really anywhere."

"So, let me understand this, because I want to be clear here. ... You're saying that often the craft or specific technical assembly sub-areas are not governed in any way? ... So what else happens in these remote area Camps? ... Did any of you actually know?"

"Experimentation on the incarcerated is completed by sub-contractors of the pharmaceutical companies. These are ongoing experiments that are constantly applied, and some of The Camps are expanding 'human testing' both here, in the Canadian facilities, and in other specific countries around the world where 'Camp industries' flourish."

The men continue eating their lunches, yet they seem somewhat moved by all the possible personal repercussions regarding these kind of 'hidden' Camp activities. … No one seems to be able to get a full grip on the dynamics of other Camp experiments discussed.

⟨5⟩

*Robert and his two friends continue working together at yet another western clay Camp facility, where their overall effort creates perfect pots, plates, jugs and other glazes extremely valuable to the **current** commercial world. Information shows that during many of the years of development, certain workers achieved 'renown' status for their fine work or by making special clay items that can sell in world markets under Camp-associated labels at enormously high prices. Yet none of the workers were aware of the value of these clay items, so as their skills developed they would be compensated not by money, but additional privileges of future 'Camp life.'*

"Cullen, have you noticed how everything keeps getting better 'privilege-wise' for all of us, within this section of the camp?"

"Yes, Robert, I know the food gets better in our section, and we get more breaks and sleep…plus less actual work time than anywhere in the Camp…perhaps slightly *more pay*."

"A fraction more pay, for sure…yet far better than years ago. … Do you think you'll ever get out? … In fact, have you ever received a date for getting out?"

All the men fall silent, yet they continue working their tasks because on the outside of the sub-Camps are large printed signs reading "**Work**

is Your Salvation." These signs, which blink on and off, are some of the main signals for the *life of the incarcerated* — they somehow give them some 'meaning.'

These Camps were originally designed specifically for separation of inmates from the general public and other inmates, yet like all 'good' inter-mixed private-government enterprises they evolved into something else. … This 'something else' usually has a different meaning from the original development design. So for many years, until Robert and his good friends 'got old,' they were allotted their 'confidence,' supported by all the good breaks. For many of the inmates this was by itself acceptable — it was a life lived and by some degree actually enjoyed.

"Since I'm an investigative social reporter, would you answer to a few of the deeper questions that you might not be able to answer so clearly if you were still in the Camp system?"

"Sure, I can answer. … I can still think clearly — that part of me hasn't changed."

"What happened to your friends Talago and Cullen? Are they still incarcerated within a Camp?"

"No, they got too old, they slowed…yet were still quite skilled. … First, Jake Cullen died…soon after went my good Talago."

"So, you are the only one of your trio left?"

"Yes, just me. … Was never really compensated for any loss since I was interned so many years ago."

"Why is that? … Have you altered that much since your initial internment?"

"Yes and no. Yes, I changed because I was a *true comrade* to two fine humans — two people who had great worth. I was part of that *friend-ship*. … It did change my perception of life and my relationship with other human beings…got me far out of my own head. And yet now, I am slowly returning to the 'internal thriller' in my own head as the fine memory of my two friends diminishes and is no more."

"Was your life worthwhile? ... Could a life of *great confinement*...a life outside of society be worthwhile?"

"Is any life not confined? Is any life not contained? What is better than a life truly shared with intimates...deep *intimates* who truly understand *the connections*?"

"Don't know the answer to that, but we can leave it for now and let the readers answer. ... Yes?"

"Maybe no one can answer your question. ... It's taken me many years to come *here*... and deal with all that was tapered in me within *The Camp*. Somehow, the isolation and punishment turned into something better — a rich *life lived...perhaps*."

"*Was it?*"

"I can argue that...and so maybe it wasn't such 'a bad turn' after all."

"Maybe...maybe not. ... I *will* write your story. ... It might just perk a brain cell or two."

"It might!" Robert exclaimed with a coy smile curving the edges of his dried lips.

Penguin

(A Love Story)

never enjoyed riding horses all that much until I rode Penguin, an old Mexican caballeros steed I discovered in a back corral of a semi-moderate resort somewhere north of Puerto Vallarta, Mexico. He was a shy rider's horse.

We settled into our full travel package resort some thirty kilometers north of Puerto Vallarta, Mexico. … It was a small accommodation, Buenas Vacaciones, with a clean environment and a moderate assortment of extras — mini-tours, good Pacific cerveza and high-quality local Ceviche served night and day.

We had never traveled together and after seven straight months of heavy dating we thought we'd give it a try. … At first it seemed quite easy to travel with Lora, an experienced Mexican traveler, yet she'd never traveled as far south as Puerto Vallarta, and never in the state of Margarette. Lora and I each loved traveling in Mexico. The coast itself and its many benefits found within the nation's various states was great — not to mention the good prices.

We walked through the bar with its wide expanse and 180-degree view of the Pacific. It was one of those places that served as a dining area, hotel entrance and general drinking accommodation. The table area that surrounded the space was filled with wonderful palms and several hundred meters of open oceanfront views — the smells, waves and the breezes were magnificent.

After settling into the room, I asked Lora if she'd like to come down to the café below with me and have our first beer...or a special Tequila drink of some kind. She was open to the suggestion and we quietly wandered down and found a table with a perfect view and ordered our first drinks.

"What do you think about this place? ... Can you compare it to your lovely Baja?"

"All I can say is, it's pretty inviting, Robert. So different from Baja... yet it certainly has a draw — a good draw for sure...."

At that point, a group of horse riders started trotting by across the main beach view, directly in front of us. Some of the animals looked quite grand, others were like shabby stray mutts...yet they all had a role...this slow passing group of horses and riders.

"You like to ride, dear lady? Have you even ridden recently?"

"In Eastern Oregon where my ex-husband and I built a ranch some years ago, we had about seven horses. We had three special ones...and I loved to trot and push them across that rugged high desert country. I also cared for them...cared a good deal."

"Most people just ride them, few seem to care for them, except the 'real' horse people. ... Caring is just as real as any part of it...eh?"

I could see her eyes clouding over, the corners seemed to redden at the thought of 'her' horses and yet not a peep more was said about her old ranch and the special horses.

"Would you like to take a little beach ride with me sometime during the week? Fact is, the horse-riding package is included. ... They keep all the horses in some corral at the back side of the property...in the silent jungle somewhere. ... So a ride tomorrow morning possibly?"

"Yes and no, Robert, or maybe ... but for now I don't want to think about it. I'd rather just look out at the ocean ...stare at the tide coming in and the colors...and drink a little Tequila."

"Yes…just relax, enjoy yourself. … We'll talk about it later. … Ride if you want…don't ride if you want. … We're here to share the whole experience…maybe a little loving included?"

"Maybe…can't say I ever pulled back from a little loving…and you seem ready. … Maybe 'up' for it most of the time since we walked on the sand?"

"Now *lovin'* has never been a bad thing during my lifetime…so 'ready' must be a perfect state — even for a wounded and fleshy Buddha."

She laughed, and her face gleamed. She was coy, yet for a second it also seemed that it was a strain for her to laugh. Maybe some restrictions left from city and recent work schedules? … I thought, *Yes, work does that, doesn't it? Yet, Lora always claimed that she loved managing the 'natural center' within a pharmacy where she'd worked during the last 13 years. There are always sculpted contradictions in people. If ever I learned anything, it is that nothing is perfectly what it seems…never. There are always alternative elements…always.*

After our drink, we settled in with all that was left to unpack in our colorful and breezy resort suite.

"I feel a little sweaty…think I'll take a cool, or maybe a *cold* shower. … In this clam-like climate, maybe colder is better?"

"I'll join you. … Would you like that?"

"Only if I can wash you…taste the tiny beads of water falling off your fine skin. … Just a little, eh?"

"Get started, I'll be there soon. … Make sure you save a tiny 'drop' of skin water for me?"

She grinned as she walked off into the little side kitchen area to prepare a small appetizer for pre-dining …some fine homemade local salsa and *queso*, and homemade hot tortilla chips.

I stripped off my clothes, jumped into the shower, and quickly lathered up most of my body. In the meantime, my imagination started working up to her lovely naked entrance.

Within five minutes and covered in soap, I heard a door close behind me. … *Yes!* I could feel her entering the large ceramic shower. Soon I felt her long fingers moving soap around my waist and pushing into my buttocks. She moved her gentle fingers in all possible directions, lightly pinching the skin ever so tenderly, then she'd dig in like a good masseuse — ever so gingerly and so deeply it felt so pleasurable.

I moved around her, washing the soap off my face as I turned to watch the tiny white soapy bubbles washing down the small openings in the shower drain. I began soaping her upper thighs, moving my hands down the soft areas of her tender and excited skin. ... I could feel the pulsing in her veins — a wanting pulse — as she pushed her lower body into my 'anxious' hands.

I felt her spread her thighs fully open to my encroaching fingers as she began breathing quite hard. ... As I continued my exploration of her upper thighs from the front and around the back side, her face expressed a wonderful pleasure. Then, as her tongue caressed my ears and tongue... I responded with moving the tip of my tongue to her lips. I could remember twitching everywhere, except at the most tender sensual spots...seemed like we were being 'saved' by each of other and blooming like the desert after a rain.

"I do love what your fingers do to my skin."

"I'm sure you've said that to many a lady."

I smiled as I slowly started pushing my fingers into those lower sensitive areas just below her fine buttocks. ... As her thighs separated even wider, I rubbed the lower section of her waiting vulva and swelling vaginal lips...so very warm almost steamy. ... I pulled her forward, letting my fingers rub everywhere...my thumbs and knuckles penetrating nudging upward and around...squeezing and pleasuring her continuously.

"Does it feel special...like it's just for you?"

She said nothing, yet her rapid breathing was a good sign of the deep pleasuring she seemed to be enjoying... voracious were her pleasures, indeed.

"I love your curves and the pulsing inside your warming womb. ... My tongue feels the path of your throbbing blood... moving faster and faster through your arteries...ah!"

Lora's body began moving to my finger's motion, darting and flowing in rhythms of play. My dancing fingers pressuring and wandering through her lower torso.

With soft fingers, she began touching the lower section of my testicles and pressing the hard muscles of my prostate gland. ... She was experienced...she knew where the pleasures were, and understood the rhythmic building of 'passions.'

I couldn't decide whether it was the deep rubbing or gentle stroking...or the special way she enfolded her fingers around the head...but for seconds the word pleasure became meaningless — 'beautiful touch' might better describe it. That certainly came closer to the feeling of 'total self-indulgence' and seemed more accurate. It it sure worked its magic!

"Slowly, I could blow so easily...*so* easily!"

"Careful...same might just be true for your lover!"

I pushed my hand softly around her torso and kept pressing everywhere inside her soft vulva. I could feel the internal passion pulsing to my advancing fingers as she groaned with pleasure. ... Her body was undulating and moving to mystical harmonies played by my soft touch. ... Her tenseness gave way to my soothing, sensual touch. She accepted me as her lover, and 'freedom came.'

Even with the soap and water flowing everywhere in our sandy ceramic shower, I could hear and feel her 'flow' and the soft culminating noise gushing in my hands. One hand deep within her body and the other wrapping around her buttocks...I could feel the tissues and the blood filling the erected semi-hard dermal tissue waltzing with my fingers to a 'Samba-like' caressing. ... *Yes!*

With special ease, she grabbed me from behind, pressed into my buttocks and slid down the front of my lower body. ... She watched my reddened, erect penis harden, pulsating and jetting upward across her nose and cheeks. She started licking the vein lines and then pushed me gently into her mouth and lapped me wildly from the lower part of my shank to the very tip of my fully *blooded* head. She seemed to want all of it at the same time. She coveted all the pleasures she aroused, so we both responded.

Yet she seemed to enjoy the deepest pleasures she gave me when using her soft fingers to play with my testicles via and her tongue at the same time. She was a most experienced woman. She had made deep love to many a lover before, yet there seemed to be a special 'level' of loving sincerity in all of her 'present' love-making…this could be felt deeply and fully understood.

Of all the times we had been together prior to the trip, our ceramic and stone shower lusting was easily the best experience yet. I was about to climax from many of the forgotten deep places within my historic body cells, it was like a group of forgotten sub-tissues which seemed to erect themselves and be near explosion — as if I were but a 23-year-old young again…finding 'free-love' times of magnificent wonder in the explosive late '60s and re-indulging with all it could bring me.

In fact, I flashed to a time with Annabelle, one of my major nine-month lovers — a woman whose supple body and mind seduced me in so many ways over many encounters. Yet she, like Lora, just craved sex… and craved it, gave and took it all, yes unifying our 'mass' together at the same time. As a constant lover from different decades I always found a proportional and equally indulged lover.

Then I felt it all moving through me and exploding into her mouth. She soon told me that was exactly what she wanted, and after my climax she kept licking me so I would remain hard. She wanted my penis to stay erect again in her tender and quieting hands. … She whispered in my ear, "Let me push you toward another erection, then I'll gently guide your 'muscle' inside me as the water continues rinsing our bodies."

"Yes, yes! Keep trying. Don't stop1 I love being this stirred up, like an old wood match being scratched before the fire."

"Go with it, love, and let me work my magic ways."

She smiled and continued playing with me as I kept rubbing and fondling her red-hard nipples, moving the tips of my fingers over them and watching them deepen in color and widen as her lovely body kept undulating to the continuous surging of my touch — a *touch* impassioned far beyond most touching I had known before. ... We were born a picture of caressing lovers practicing the 'old ways.'

Finally, we slipped out of the great ceramic shower to a small lover's lounge chair where she lapped and licked me until my erection rose again, hard enough for yet another full indulgence. She slowly and precisely climbed atop me, taking her vulva with all her power halfway on the penis and then pulling upward with all possible clamping. Pulling upwards and out, moving in all directions in a kind of Brazilian sensual dance like those in the cinema coming from the dancing drummers of Rio during Mardi Gras. I pulled her down closer to me pressing her hard breasts and bring her erect nipples to my mouth — my tongue doing all it could to lick and keep her fired-up.

We stayed and swayed together, and her body rose and bucked like a wild horse about to kick and suddenly climaxed with passion beyond any...she screamed out in bounteous sensual delight and fell on top of my chest as I once again climaxed once more during her full powerful indulgence. She pulled me in so deeply as she wanted to feel the semen flow into her womb...shooting so deeply within her...she looked up at me and joyfully smiled.

"Now that was a sweet set of little pleasures!"

We lay together, with her on top and both of us sweating hard for several minutes. Lora nearly relaxed enough to sleep, before she said, "Let's lay naked together in the large bed, and let the ceiling fan circle its breezes on us. And then possibly some sleep...yes?"

"Yes, I'd love to lay next to your lovely and loving body on that big bed...some needed sleep and maybe more later...eh?"

We lay there, exhausted after our wondrous lovemaking, and each quickly fell asleep. ... A nap under the spinning fan blades always felt fine.

The next morning, I was at the breakfast bar ordering some *huevos* and hot sausage with a glass of lime Mimosa on the side. ... I was alone until our new friends (to be) sat down at the table next to me — a large fully bearded, red headed man along with a redheaded, freckled woman and a pretty 40-something brunette. The man was an old crab captain named Raymond Owens, along with his wife Maureen, and his sister Eden. They became our close friends for the next six drinking and partying days. Yes, they were as close as Santa Barbara party folk could be.

Raymond Owens was a crab boat skipper out of Crescent City, California, still netting Dungeness crab after an absence of eight years when he was in federal prison accused of cocaine smuggling. His ship's hold had hid 10,000 kilos of fine Colombian cocaine and good Captain Raymond was captured on the high seas coming near San Diego. The U.S. Coast Guard had stopped him and put the whole crew in prison and confiscated the booty.

Once directly nabbed at sea by the U.S. Coast Guard his expensive lawyers went into instant plea bargain action for the good captain. He got eight years, which did include certain required testimony of which the good captain said little — he just told stories.

Raymond was a large man with gray peppering his red beard. His age was somewhere in the late 50s. Beneath his drinking and laughing lurked a very 'rough' character — an experienced crab ship captain who loved his way of life yet the 'dance of the leprechaun' was in his heart, as the Irish contend.

Raymond had divorced his second wife of 25 years and married his 10-year mistress, Maureen Ives. She was a smart, pleasant soul who laughed and smiled a lot. Raymond also often traveled with his rich sister, Eden Hughes, from Santa Barbara, as he had on this trip to western Mexico.

Eden was celebrating her recovery from severe breast cancer treatment, though her numbers were still quite high. Still bald from the cancer therapy, Eden was a strong woman who could deal with most anything — a sparkling gem of a female. Her husband had died two years prior and she'd inherited a 150-year old California ranch and the fortune he made in the oil industry.

Prior to Lora coming down to the dinner area, the four of us jabbered, guffawed and chatted, sharing many plates of fresh ceviche followed by good beer. ... We were fast friends on the beach and maybe we could dance through a few 'side-trips' together while at the resort. Might just be part of our shared futures.

Lora entered the conversation and sat down to my right, immediately taking up pleasant conversation with Eden and Maureen. These were congenial and open people with whom we could partake in many enjoyable days at the beach and *nothing* beyond that purpose, as I would eventually come to realize. Trips of any kind can often have unintended lessons, if one actually reads the fine cues. Few of us do that though, we just keep marching blindly to the next eventual vacation.

"So, Raymond, you're back to crab fishing after an eight-year suspension?"

"Yeah, Robert, it's the only thing I know except of course drinking, eating and smoking weed, and of course good sex — the best of which is kindly provided by the good red-headed lady to my left!"

"So many compliments, captain. I might start to 'shy up' over it"

"Honey...never saw you shy up over anything — ever. ... Not once!"

Eden grabbed her beer and snatched a few nachos, adding fresh salsa and placing them on the tabletop in front. She directed her next words to Lora. "So, first trip to Puerto Vallarta you say?"

"Yes, I spend most of my time in several different parts of Baja when I travel to Mexico previously...loved the beaches, snorkeling, the tasty food...especially seafood — just like this wonderful ceviche...just fine."

"I've been down to Vallarta about seven times, sometimes with lovers, sometimes with my former husband and a few times with my brother Raymond, sitting across the table from me."

"What did you do, Eden, when he was in prison...your brother I mean?"

"Wrote him, laughed a lot, traveled to other places...got married twice...divorced twice...got breast cancer and was treated two times."

Lora looked at her and surprised me by lifting her bar glass to the sophisticated Eden. She raised her glass in a toast...and the two women touched glasses.

"And then again, Lora, I give a toast to all the good men I've known, including my best friend and brother, Raymond, who always stood there for me...all the time...every time!"

"Nice to have a sibling that solid in your life. ... Most of mine are usually lost somewhere in other states, other moods, and one just 'screwed up' and was a screw up — a victim of everything in life *one inch at a time.*"

I was quite surprised to see Lora open up so fast, she was a shy person in the traditional Western way, though not about sensual talk...not shy about that at all...yet seemingly about most everything else.

The evening continued for several hours with laughing and drinking, and some eating until we all decided to jump into the Pacific, which was about a hundred meters from us pounding its August rhythms against the vast beachhead.

When night came, we all decided to take one of the resort tours together. ... The five of us would venture to San Blas. ... Lora seemed quite pleased with our new friends.

Later that night, in bed, we chatted about how lucky we were to meet such *genuine* people on such a short Mexican vacation. ... Good souls they were...or certainly seemed to be.

{2}

The next morning 'drifting' in the early orange sun I wandered behind the resort property to see what other possible adventures I could dive into. ... Several hundred meters walking into the deeper jungle section of the property, I saw a cut within the trees and there I found a small corral. Within the corral built into the greenway and shrubs was a muddy but finely constructed open stable. I walked the acreage and in the back end found a small palomino and standing next to the older horse was a caballero calling himself Panchito. He was known as an old wrangler and had been hired by the resort to tend to the animals — horses, mules, donkeys and whatever else they kept for the guests. Panchito was a white-bearded man in his late 70s…his skin was leather rough and tan. Anyone could see that he was a man who lived a hard yet very real outside life.

"I'd like to take a horse out *mañana, señor. ¿Es esto posible?*"

"*Sí, señor, bueno.* … Which *caballo* would you like…a squeaky wild one or an easy horse…or something *en el medio?*"

The old man was coy and easygoing, and he seemed to like to play a little bit with tourists' minds. Yet he did everything right — he was accommodating to the extreme. I started to move carefully around the horses. I was a little hesitant and cautious, but intelligent about it all. … I wanted to ride again after a 20-year absence.

I had pulled back from horses after a large Paint that was classified 'very gentle' had run away with me. Yes, I was almost thrown beneath two trees, and had near misses along outstretched tree branches that passed quickly as the young Paint forced her way back to the home stable. It took two large wranglers and a strong cowgirl to slow the horse, whose name was Old Timer. Never would forget that experience. It happened at one of the best and most classy stables in Southern California — Rancho Santa Fe.

"You want a good horse, smart horse, yet very gentle? … Sometimes, *señor,* that kind of horse may be old. … *¿Está bien?*"

"Yes, like this lovely old Palomino in the muddy back corral. … Why is he alone, *señor?*"

"Many of the other horses are much younger, so they reject him… avoid the old Palomino!"

"Sounds like too much of human society these days. Indeed, age puts many of us in back mud-holes. Too many put out to pasture forever… what's waiting for this horse I imagine. … Hopefully he doesn't end up as horse meat in some home stew, eh?"

The old man knew what I was saying; yet I could see he loved the horses. Emotion stirred across his leathery face. ... He said nothing in words, his expressions said much more.

"So, should I fix up that old horse for you? ... Penguin, that's his name. ... You like to ride him? ... You like old Penguin?" The old man smirked at me. He seemed to be proud of my choice yet mocking it at the same time, but I could see right through his expression — if any tourists took that horse out, he could live longer, and the old man could then take care of him.

So much passed between us in silence...feelings expressed without words. ... In short bursts of the two different languages, the old man and I *truly* understood each other.

"So, *señor*, you want me to get Penguin ready *ahora?*"

"No...No...I'll come down about...well after lunch tomorrow. ... I'll be taking old Penguin for a trot on the beach, along with a couple of other folks...*entender?*"

"*Sí, señor. Come y luego ve a buscar a Penguin mañana.*"

The next day during our chatting, the two central women in the good crab Captain's party also decided they wanted to ride horses on the beach with me. So 'in the plot,' Lora and Captain Raymond would stay on the beach and drink and laugh together while they watched us 'trot' by.

I eventually sauntered off to the back area of the resort through a short jungle path to the horse corrals. ... I was pleased with myself, Penguin and my desire to ride the surf-filled beaches of this Pacific coast playground. Interestingly, I was about to embark on another 'gentle' ride on an easy horse. Hopefully *Penguin* would not surprise me and might keep the concept of 'easy ride' in tack.

⟨4⟩

The next day, we traveled towards San Blas with Captain Raymond, his wife, and the 'sparkling' Eden. .... Eden was like a jungle flower in perfect bloom — colorful, alive, fragrant and always touching the sun. Together on the short trip we enjoyed the 'quiet' local food, ancient sites, swims in small lakes and pools with small crocodiles caged off in a marine reptile area managed by the Mexican government and the University of Nayarit. It all seemed simple and inexpensive, all powered by local labor...managed solely by underpaid workers, students, and biological scientists from the University.

Nevertheless, the sights were wonderful and the weather quite pleasant. The cool-water swimming was refreshing and the company generally fine. During the trip to San Blas, Lora and I seemed like renewed lovers 'awakened' and the sparks of 'unite more' seemed to be popping off once again.

We also traveled to a small zoo and unique aquatic area just inside San Blas. Our conversations were glowing and the atmosphere was vibrant, particularly on the way back — maybe because of the sun's intense power all were nearly in utter silence. ... Most of us in the open van just stared out into the jungle, watching the many shadows dance towards dusk. Every day it seemed like the orange sun with its yellow and purple casts blazed just above the 'green' landscape of assorted palms and giant leaves filling our wondering visions.

At the resort, we said our nightly goodbyes for the evening once we stepped off the van, and all seemed to be happy to either sleep or maybe jot down to the bar for more beer and free Ceviche.

Lora and I watched the last vestiges of the sun setting, and then glanced into each other's eyes deeply. ... *Ah, the joy of reawakened love on an exquisite day's end.*

"How about a short walk to the lovely rock caves on the north side of the property before we eat?"

"Sounds like an idea, Robert...a good idea. ... I'm somewhat exhausted but I could go for that...yes!"

Lora was the kind of person who rarely made definite statements, yet somehow, I always seemed to fully understand what she meant, even when she seemed rather subtle. She was always coy and there was a certain 'youth' about her — the opposite of her physical age. ... Then again for most of us above a certain age, age itself has very little relevance... and in particular, *none* between lovers...especially when the loving is still vibrant and 'brand new' a good deal of the time. ... That was how it was between us...yes, most of the time.

We held hands and played with each other's fingers while strolling down the path toward a group of caves beyond the north beach end of the resort. These caves always filled at high tide, which was coming very soon. ... We climbed up the rocks, some of it was simple and some of the climbing was more difficult. ... A few of the areas we climbed through were pure shale as we continued advancing towards a gray sand colored platform at cliff top in front of the giant caves.

The ocean noise behind us was extremely loud as we began exploring the small shallow rooms in the cave. One room, a large one, stood out as exceptional.

I asked Lora if she remembered the second week of our affair, some eight months before, when we were both alone in the water at the lake, naked below our waists? We'd stood that way for a while, facing each other in that lake water at the beginning of a warm spring. The lake was called Squaw. Not a great name at all but a wonderful freshwater paradise with few people ever there, especially in spring.

She smiled coyly and said, "Yes, I remember our holding each other by the shoulders and making love in the cold water — stripped from the waist down...beautiful vision.

"I enjoyed the time spent, shaping you into me, playing with you via my fingertips as you entered me...so excited, large and engorged you were. ... Yes, I remember it all quite well."

"That was one of the best, most physically exciting events I can remember...I can almost feel your fingertips touching everywhere... your soft fingers did a fine job *pressing the pleasure zones.*"

"I can do that again. ... You were also there for me, your soft, strong fingers everywhere and beyond. You touched places that brought me back to my *hippie youth* — joyful indeed, Robert."

We saw no one anywhere, no one. … The fond remembrance of our lovemaking 'like fantasy' and being alone was more than enough to get each of us going — naturally in different ways, yet we were both right there in our heads, both ready…and of course it started.

We quickly fondled each other's bodies, locked lips and tongues, slowly stripping each other as the waves pounded loudly near the cave's entrance. For each of us, fingers and tongues seemed to travel to each tender portion of the other's body. … I petted and responsively loved her breasts taking the nipples deeply into my mouth, at the same time I pushed them into my face sucking and licking them as passionately as ever. … Then she dropped down and started playing with my inner thighs which she did so well, then quickly taking the head of my penis into her mouth licking at all sections of my blooded and engorged organ…moving around all sensitive spots with her hands, lapping the top section and the head so vigorously, in-between with her eyes she watched the organ rise higher and stiffer to her touch, instinctive secret tactile pleasures using her tongue and fingers together…yes!

"Right now, Robert, I need you deep in my womb…very deep… remain as stiff and as hard as you can…stay that way for a while, eh?"

"I will dear love, yes I will…hopefully this will be something very special for each of us…something deeply inspired…"

I smiled and guided her slowly to the floor of the cave and she ended up on all fours as I gently entered from behind and above pushing and twisting, sliding and snuggling, pounding and thrusting, giving her more and more in several directions within her open and burning inner-womb. Our coitus was nearly simultaneous, mini-seconds apart from her time to mine…she moved her neck upward staring into the cave ceiling above her…'ah a massive web colony of tiny spiders eh…then she grabbed her bathing suit and started laughing regarding the spiders, and watched me in my naked dance with raging multiple emotions exploding…also laughing *with her* in a highly emotional and releasing manner…we laughed hysterically. Sometimes the humor of the moment seems far more outrageous in *particular* times and situations, where at other times it could never quite happen that way....

The ocean started to burst, blazing white foam crashed everywhere around the cave's entrance, and so we hustled (still laughing) towards the path and headed down...we continued pushing downward in explosive laughter as the two 'cave lovers' stumbled their way back to the beach resort and our new friends.

⟨5⟩

All the group, Raymond, Eden, Maureen and Lora sat together drinking and laughing at the large cabana table which was (of course) right against the beachfront as I joined them. Lora was always quiet, always reserved but did seem to enjoy laughter and drink, Ceviche and other good seafood.

"Eden, I'm beginning to enjoy this trip...maybe it's all the drink and laughter...sometimes I truly miss laughter."

Eden looked across at Lora, smiled, grabbed a Pacifico beer and downed half the bottle followed by another smile and several chips more of Ceviche and salsa.

"Lora, you stay on the beach long enough and it all just becomes 'home'...as it grabs you again and again...."

Raymond drank two beers as we talked. He was an enormous red-bearded man who played as hard as he worked, and this was his time for play.

"Eden, should I share a little of that 'special stuff' with Lora and Robert, think they'd enjoy it?"

"I do, Lora seems like she may have had a good deal of it in the past...!"

"And what is the stuff you're talking about, Raymond...?"

"Just some fine 'private stock' something anyone from your time would remember, and still indulge in?"

"Occasionally I still 'do hits' but only with pure stuff almost organic… the best of all weed available…"

"This my dear is masterful as good as it gets from a prime dealer… trader would be more appropriate…sea trader…and Colombia is where this batch arrived from…fine indeed…maybe better than fine."

Maureen sat down at the large beach table and smiled at Lora after kissing his sister and Raymond. Somehow, she always seemed confident and quite pleased with herself.

"Raymond must have offered you and your mate some of our 'good stuff'?"

"Yes, and sometime later I will take him up on it…maybe tomorrow!"

Just at that moment a group of six sauntering horses passed by not far from us on the beachfront, with each animal trotting in single file. The second horse was the old black and white Pinto Robert rode…and ride he did…like a classic Western rider from an old fifties film low he was and pushed back in the stirrups easy and 'at ease' in the saddle. Everyone at our table stared at the group of horses passing by on this surf pounding beachfront…somehow these horses represented an almost classical historical beauty… Later, dusk was coming as the riders returned trotting against the setting sun and blazing tropical colors of orange re-dish gold which created a wonderful picture…a fine 'print' emblazoned across the beachscape. At first, we didn't realize that Robert was on his old Pinto, then he alone stopped on the beachfront, turned his horse towards our group and waved then turned old 'Penguin' again and rode into the surf front and tried to catch up with the other riders.

"That Robert is one hell of a rider, Lora…never seen a human so easy in the saddle, kinda looks like professional wrangler."

Lora drank more of her beer, took a chip or two covered in fire beer, and just smiled at Eden.

"Never told me he was such a 'gallant' rider…rides classically I'd say?"

"Yes, looks like he's riding down old Dodge in the 1870s…or maybe Deadwood."

Then Maureen commented about Robert and his ride, because as she explained to the group she grew up on a cattle ranch in South Dakota and she'd experienced what a man looked like when 'calm' atop his mount… and was quite sure Robert was one of those 'true' riders. The group was still laughing and drinking as Robert walked up to the table…he kissed Lora on the back of her neck and slowly moved his fingers further down massaging as he went…

"Have a drink, Robert…you looked great on that Pinto against the surf…"

"Thanks…haven't ridden for some time because of a 'crazy' run away horse, yet today somehow I wanted to ride again, and I really like old Penguin…that's the horse's name…Penguin."

Raymond called the waiter over and asked him to bring mass *"Ceviche and cinco cervezas. Cinco me amigo. … Cinco por favor."*

"Some fine horse riding, Robert. I personally enjoyed it as I downed good beer…enjoyed it from right here!"

"Don't like riding, Raymond? … Did you ever ride much?"

"Not much, the only place I like riding is in the sack, or on the crab boat…otherwise I'm not an animal rider…period."

Maureen looked over at Raymond, then grabbed his hand and smiled at the group looking somewhat proud.

"He does love a *good* animal ride, yes he does, and my strong thighs can bring him what he enjoys…at least during the last fifteen years."

"I'd drink to that dear lady…drink to that…knocked me out of two bad marriages it did…just for that ride…no better!"

"Well for me I could say…a good healthy rocking rider is hard to find!"

"And again, for me, glad for that, happy you are there…drinks up?"

The sun had almost set as the lights of the resort started to take over and the band members coming out and setting up their wares for the evening's entertainment. Lora and Robert clinked their glasses and Maureen and Raymond waved goodbye to the group and set off to their suite for the evening…somewhat snookered.

⟨7⟩

Wandering through the town of Pequeno Central we were surprised at the vast number of silver jewelry stores…one craftsman owner was just that much better than the next one. Maureen, Eden and I wandered everywhere in the town counting on the sharp Spanish of Eden to keep us going when poor-quality stuff was somewhat ill-defined and not easy to recognize.

Back at the resort, Lora and Raymond had beach lunch waiting for the three of us to return from shopping within the next two hours. Both of them started to drink, downing a few lime blended Margaritas one after another. … Suddenly Raymond asked Lora to his suite for a toke of some of the finest and most expensive 'bud' she could ever smoke… anywhere in southern Mexico.

After three drinks, her deep past started to creep on her quickly, including a vow she made to all her children 'not to ever smoke' but all that was needed was a good salesman to creep up on her and put it back into her mind. So she accepted the old crab captain's offer. The two of them went off to his beach suite to 'toke some' from Raymond's 'special' pipe…a pipe for pure happiness he called it. … Lora smiled with some hesitation.

I made a decision when shopping to buy Lora a fine pair of exquisite earrings which were over 50 years old and finely handcrafted of upgraded silver from the old El Grande mine in central Mexico not that far us. It had closed in the late '70s. The earrings were long, hanging and pierced. They sloped perfectly for Lora's head and finely proportioned neck. So, the owner and I bargained and Eden got into it. Finally a 'fair' price was reached…at least fair as far as I could count on.

The craftsman's assistant wrapped the earrings and put them in a small box. The exchange was then finalized, with all involved seemingly content.

"Such lovely thin silver earrings, Robert. I'm sure Lora will be quite pleased."

"Yes, I do expect her to be pleased, Eden. … I'd be overjoyed if I got something like these beauties."

"That is, pleased if you were a lovely woman like Lora?"

"No, pleased on all accounts because if I got them for myself I know that I could toss them on the ears of another fine lady."

"Harsh, dear Robert. So earthly and pragmatic you seem."

"If you'd seen or dated as many women as I had in the last six years, then you might just feel the same way, Maureen."

Coyly she smiled with her hard green eyes glowing as she tossed her long red hair and moved her fingers through to tighten all visible hair around her forehead.

"Time for us to head back to the resort and see how the others are doing, right?"

We walked along the beach and after about two kilometers we entered the north section of the resort. We discovered Raymond sitting at a beach table, talking to the dinner hostess and the salsa dance instructor. He smiled at us as we approached him and sat down at his table. … The hostess and the instructor instantly smiled, and both were soon off in another direction.

"How about some beer or margaritas to go all around…or anything else? … I am the generous captain tonight."

We all agreed to have a drink of some kind, and as we waited for the order I asked Raymond where Lora was.

"Last time I saw her she was heaving up and smack against our bathroom door…never came out. She didn't sound great."

"Was she sick or something?"

"I don't know, but you can go into the room right now and check it out if you like. … She sure seemed to love 'the smoke'…maybe too much. Eh?"

I looked at him for a moment as if he were kidding and yet I knew he wasn't. A crab boat captain drug distributor he'd been, a smuggler who'd lost most of his connections. When people get *obscured* in anything, that usually happens. So he seemed distant…aloof…drank too much and smoked too much.

I quickly worked my way to the captain's suite, opened the door, saw nothing and heard little, so I knocked on the closed bathroom door to get some kind of a sound in the room. … I heard nothing other than my knock, so I pounded on the door. Then I heard someone regurgitating into something…probably the toilet.

When I opened the bathroom door, Lora was laying on the floor almost unconscious. … I quickly grabbed the back of her head and raised it up gently. Her eyes opened and she, waiting for moments, spoke slowly. "I'm feeling quite sick."

"What happened to you? Did you drink too much, or was it something else? … I smell pot or a combination of it and something else… too much of all of it, period!"

She nodded her head, slowly turned over on her knees and raised herself to the bowl, and then heaved-up another time. As she vomited, I held her head and stroked and smoothed her hair. I talked gently to her for the next 95 minutes, until Eden came to the door and asked if she could help.

"Yes, I'd appreciate some old-fashioned help. She won't agree to move up to our suite, nor will she let me call a doctor or take her to a local hospital."

"All right. … Let me see if I can talk to her…then maybe we'll try to move her. I'll let you know when and you can help me."

As soon as I left the room, Lora panicked and called out to me quite anxiously and madly asking me to stay. … She demanded that I not leave her at all. I told her that I'd be going nowhere until I saw her safely tucked in bed in our suite, ready to sleep and not vomiting. Her eyes closed again quietly. … I could see an expression of fear relax as Eden and I helped her out of Raymond's suite and up to ours on the second floor of the old hacienda building.

After about a half-hour and with some difficulty getting her undressed and into bed, Eden washed her face and then laid a cold rag her forehead.

… She was very patient and kind. Within minutes Lora asked her to leave and she went immediately back to her own suite.

For another hour, I sat next to Lora holding her hand and head. Every time I attempted to get up, she grabbed my hand and pulled me back asking me desperately *not to leave her,* then requested that I continue to stay.

"Don't leave me! … Please, stay with me! … *Please!*"

There was a deep desperation in her cry that seemed to be buried within her soul somewhere beyond this place. … There was a silent understanding in her plea. Another hour went by as I stood just behind her sleeping head, feeding her cold water when I could or gently rubbing it on her sweat-reddened lips with my fingertips. Finally, when I was sure she was sleeping, I got up, looked at the time and decided to trek down to dinner before they stopped serving it.

I exited the room and stepped out in silence, looking back at Lora sleeping quite peacefully. I thought I'd get her some soda or something easy on her stomach, and come back to the room immediately. … *Maybe I could go down and eat quickly with the group? Maybe 20 minutes and then get back to our suite? … That should be all right,* I thought.

So, I fleetly ran down the stairs and headed to the open dining room. … I ordered steak-ranchero, brown rice and black beans. I was hungry by that time…nearly famished. Heading to the beach soon after me were Raymond, Maureen and Eden. … They grabbed a table near me and started ordering their usual stuff. … I had the waiter move me over to their larger table and we all started laughing, drinking, yapping and eating.

"How's Lora doing up in the suite?"

"She's totally knocked out and sleeping like a lamb."

"Is that right?"

"Yeah, Eden. Lora was really out, eyes closed, obviously asleep… dead-like when I left the room for a quick bite of food."

At that point with everyone laughing and enjoying themselves. Maureen suddenly stopped and looked across at the bar…her faced seemed surprised, almost shocked.

"Isn't that your Lora sitting at the circular bar?"

"Impossible!"

"Not so, my dear boy. …Not so!"

I turned my head briefly and glanced at a well- dressed woman sitting at the far end of the resort bar. It did look like her, but the face was somewhat blurred at the approximate one hundred meters distance. So, I got up and headed toward the bar to meet this *nightclub* dressed woman sitting contented and alone. She was dressed to 'the tee.' … Damn what I was seeing? Somehow she got here, but how?

As I approached her, I said, "Hello, Lora. … What are you doing here?"

With a look of ingested poison beaming from her eyes — resentment so deep it was hard to understand, yet it all pointed and was directly at me — she said, "You will dance only with me tonight. … No one else!"

I was slightly taken aback by her sharp commands. … Nothing else but her reddened tongue could I see…yet her voice, her eyes, her stare were all focused directly on me with key-in military artillery sighting.

"Sure, my dear…I'll dance with you and only with you all night."

She must have been hurting inside, she made her 'needed points' her stoic points, but she was sure in some kind of pain, way beyond me. "No one but me, Robert. … No one but me, *all night!*"

Well we danced, sang, re-worked our moves and learned a new Salsa routine that night. … And, we continued to drink on…Lora less than before, but she did imbibe a bottle of beer or two. …Yet at that point, all I could consider was my great surprise at her just being there. I was even more taken in by who she'd become in such a short time…a blinding sublimated alternation indeed.

⟨6⟩

The next day we were all on a short tour of San Blas, a small inlet town north of the resort. It was one of the ancestral homes of the Huichol Indians. A colorful people whose interconnected Gods were well represented by the bitter and 'dream-oriented' peyote root and the multicolored cactus surrounding them.

After seeing some minor, yet robbed ancient ruins, we drove toward our main destination — a small internal river and its surrounding inhabited wetland areas where the State of Nayarit had built a small wildlife sanctuary and a cool river swimming area for tourists.

This area was surprisingly clean and peaceful, filled with rare jungle plants and assorted flowering horticulture…a romantic and enjoyable place — if erotic was one's game. And with that kind of charm anywhere one travels, it can be yes at times and at other times no. … Rarely is romance neither…it's always emotions fighting for balance.

Lora looked fine, especially around water and in her dark blue bathing suit. Her near blond gray hair was a wondrous picture near the aqua blue sky, streams and ponds filled with floating wild orchids. Lora was a fine swimmer and enjoyed water, so she was immediately off to swim in the cool pond waters. On this day, a very warm day even by Mexican standards, the cold gentle pools seemed even more inviting.

I could see natural cut coves within the stream and jungle structure where I thought some additional loving might just erase the deepest of angers. Isn't it often true how we imagine many things which 'could be' better than the present state of affairs seem to be, yet men are driven by powerful epigenetic forces deeper derived than most humans could ever imagine.

In the year preceding the trip, I had accomplished a good deal of 'self' oriented research into wide evolutionary biology, so I had a better than average grip on evolutionary development. … Yet in many ways, it all breaks down to 'current' procrastination-type connections…always confronting one.

In these wonderful cooling waters, I approached Lora as I did many other times where we swam together in various other small lakes in Washington State. Yes, many a good time did we have in those pristine lakes and ponds, moving at times and at others dancing in the waters and pressing body against body, loving on and off sometimes for hours…like a joyful dance of Mallards in heat. … We were two souls pleasuring each other in a natural set of sensual connections in a kind of 'pure orgasmic experience' that we joyfully shared. So, we found a shadow space where several currents and streams came together and where the pressure of the water acted concurrently on our excited rhythmic bodies to enhance our coitus.

Lora was one who said little, yet she had experienced many lovers through the sequence of her life. … Each one of these experiences she appreciated and acknowledged, though she never stated any of this in verbal ways…never discussed loving even as the wild 'fleshy' committed lover she was.

It always started slowly, with a couple of easy kisses on the neck, as I moved my hands around her backside, managing to press my fingers and knuckles in and around her most exposed dermal tissues and deeper areas of her vaginal sensuality.

For fifteen minutes or so we worked our bodies up a couple of degrees only to 'succumb' to the cooling waters around us. … She quickly dropped the bottom part of her suit then slowly pulled my trunks down to the lowest quarter of my body. She made sure that I was as hard as possible, and at the height of excitement she grabbed me and pushed me inside her as she lifted up and quaked with internal joy. I rose higher inside her, moving from side to side within her, in all parts of her loving womb. Then she squeezed me and pulled me deeper, using the sucking and clamping power of her inner muscles. … I couldn't remember being more worked up, more excited, **never before was it that much** even in the cold waters of our Washington lakes. … *Ah…such utter rapture!*

"Stay up…keep it up…let it all pour into me. … I'll give you the same, many times over, before your *little* explosion."

I was lost indeed in the drawing rhythms of her swaying and pulling, her glorious tender lovemaking. … She performed as my lover, even after her recent distance and estrangement. And she did give me all she could as a 'giver' at that moment she was my tryst as few others were, and the cool waters just added to our loving. ... *Yes!* So lost was I in her steaming womb, I could barely speak — and for me that was quite unusual.

"Ready are you? ... I can feel the blood pulsing, the magic pounding aggressively within me...a sharing for us. ... Surprised, are you?"

"Yes, surprised by the 'gift' you're giving me — especially after yesterday...and yet your eyes."

"My eyes make me an even better lover — even the day after I awake to the 'rise,' dear amour...so enjoy."

"Yes indeed, dear lady...yes indeed."

She drew our bodies closer again as the flowing cooler currents pressed us from behind and we climaxed perfectly in tune. This was exactly what Lora wanted and was quite able to fulfill. ... After, we stood there gently and deeply kissing each other, then few seconds later another dual climax followed and we, for a short time were one, at least our senses told us that...beyond our rationalselves.

"Nice, eh? ... You feel fully satisfied? ... Better?"

"So damned better...as I would hope you do too."

Lora smiled, grabbed my hand and pulled me toward her once again...then we swam to a little sandy beach area about 200 meters from our private undercurrent-fed cove. We slowly moved toward our companions, holding hands and smiling like two young lovers exiting an opium den. Two shining stars we were in an Old World painting.

All five of us, all our friends were quiet as the van passed through some of the local villages and homes along this curving jungle road, and for us maybe because of 'all the good loving' little was said and the utter hot silence of late day remained, except for the occasional call of a cockatoo or green parrot.

As the van wound its way down the road, Lora held my hand quite tightly — her fingers moving and intertwining continually. So, our hands danced quietly within the space of our twirling and heated grips as the van moved up the road toward the setting western sun.

⟨7⟩

In the early morning filtered sun, I set out once again down the back path toward the corral that held Penguin. When I got to an outside gate, the old man laughed again as I requested Penguin. ... "Penguin, ah-ha." He barely contained his smirk as he suggested in Spanish that I could find him in the back stall behind all the other horses. We exchanged a few short, light sentences in Spanish and English and I jotted off to find my old friendly horse, Mr. Penguin.

As I turned the corner in the back corral area, there were two small ponies in a short stall and then a long fenced in area leading toward Penguin in the back stalls. He was eating some green hay by himself. As he ate, he gently turned his old head toward me as I approached. He seemed content and at ease, plus he seemed to appreciate *any* presence. I waited for him to finish his meal as the old Vaquero came up behind me and said, *"¿Quieres viajar a Penguin hoy? ¿Sí?'*

"*Sí, señor,* I would appreciate you getting him ready for the ride...we will be coming in from the other direction...*entiende?"*

"*Sí, señor, Penguin. Sí.* I'll get him ready."

He quickly bridled and saddled Penguin then asked me if I'd wait in the front area of the corral, *"Está bien para montar con las tres mujeres?"* he asked, since he'd set me up to ride with three new guests — Sharon, Millie and Rita. I nodded and he proceeded.

As we waited around for the old vaquero to get things ready, I discovered that one of the women, Rita, had a ranch in Kansas with her sister, plus she owned several horses and rode quite a lot. In fact, when Rita was much younger she competed in rodeo roping, barrel racing and calf roping contests. ... She knew how to handle horses well. I guessed that I'd learn something from her for sure...plus she had quite a trim figure and great personality, making her the compete package.

The other women had been friends since high school. Millie was a somewhat overweight nurse, and a poor rider. Sharon said little except that she had also ridden for years and worked in pharmaceutical marketing.

"Robert's the name and I'm pleased to ride along with you all."

"As you know, I'm Millie, and I can say the same. We're pleased to have you along, Robert."

We all kept chatting with each other as we rode along up a northern ridge, then climbed up and then back down to the beach area below a second hill. We had to zigzag up and sideways over the worst parts of the ridge. The most difficult part of the ride, in fact, was the descent. In this last section, we also had to take the horses over some large, smooth and slippery rocks. This was not easy and it scared Millie, but this path was the only way to the beach on the other side of what I assumed to be a dry, but at seasonal times flowing creek bed leading to the Pacific.

Sharon was a pretty good rider and she stayed a good deal ahead, moving along with Rita. Millie and I were third and fourth on the rough trail. Penguin was beautiful and strong on the path, and every step we took was solid as I figured it would be. ... He was steady, never excited and handled the ocean spray-slicked rocks like a mule.

Millie was having problems and her horse, Camille, was slipping and jockeying on the stones and getting more nervous and edgy with each step. ... I had certainly experienced these signs before. ... Finally, Camille stopped and refused to go forward. Millie seemed anxious and somewhat scared, so I dismounted and led Camille slowly across the slippery surface. I asked Millie to lead Penguin as I walked her horse to the edge of the path where the wide flow of smooth rocks ended.

"Thanks, Robert, I was getting a little shaky sitting on that edgy horse."

"Yes...glad the horse obliged me and followed nicely."

By that time Rita and Sharon rode up to us to see exactly what was going on and why we were so far behind. Millie explained what happened, they all thanked me, and then Rita asked me to ride at her side as we rode on the sandy beach and into the surf.

"I do appreciate you helping my friend, Robert. That was a decent thing to do. … Not all men these days would do that…few in fact."

"Guess I'm just a product of another age. … That's just who I am. … Anyway it was nothing really."

"I'm going to give you my personal cell number, and if you come down to Kansas anytime, call me. You can come and stay with my sister and me on our ranch. … Maybe we can ride some?"

"Thanks, I just might take you up on that. … You are one hell of a rider…an excellent rider, indeed."

We all rode on, talking about Kansas and the Midwest and our experiences with animals present and past. Then we moved to an easy trot on the hard sand near the surf. … It was quite remarkable and exhilarating.

Once again, we rode past the resort heading due south. This time no one was at the bar and no one was eating, so the four of us just rode past the area and continued to chat and ride until early evening. … Finally, I found my tired legs climbing the stairs to our suite and I stepped in the main room just a few minutes prior to dinner.

⟨8⟩

On the night prior to our departure, we learned short versions of Salsa and Merengue dancing, and we drank, danced, ate and discussed many 'minor things' all through the late hours of the evening. That night Maureen, Raymond and Eden were just wonderful, lite and charming… seemingly as close to us as new friends could be, and as a short interval in life could allow. Even I, usually conservative about newfound friends, found myself letting my guard down. … It was made easier with all the good food, drink, beer and dancing…easy for sure. At the very end of the evening, Maureen and Raymond invited us to share some of their "best stuff" in their suite.

"Got some fine 'stuff' this morning, Robert and Lora. … Fine pure 'hash' from eastern Brazil I believe."

"That's great, we'll visit you after a quick night-cap, hopefully, if lovely Lora feels like it."

"We'll see how I feel. ... I did have a problem the other night...but I'm totally over it."

It was that "special" way in which Lora expressed herself — "totally over it" — somehow there seemed to be more buried in her brief words than what was on the surface.

As the evening closed out, Lora and I danced again, slowly, to several more tunes. ... Tender dancing to the automatic music system the hotel crew turned on prior to leaving. ... Only the two of us and another couple remained, as we all seemed to want to squeeze as much pleasure out of the last night's stay as we could.

Later, Lora and I lay in the bed together in the suite, each of us having taken a brief shower alone just before. ... We were getting relaxed prior to our ride to the plane for the States at ten in the morning. As I had already guessed, Lora was not in any mood to smoke anything again. ... There was nothing to forgive...when she said, "Not tonight," regarding a last possible exchange with Raymond and Maureen in their suite. As Lora rolled to the side in her lovely white transparent silk slip, all her very womanly body was exposed under the dim lights in our room.

I moved over toward her and put my hand on her right hip and she said in a soft manner, "Hey, I'm a little tired...not tonight. Okay?"

I said nothing, excited as I was about her, and just clicked the light off and thought it was all too much for her after her "little sickness" two *not so easy* nights prior. So, with ease I listened to the beautiful ocean breezes flowing through the linen curtains of our large windows...and then watched the beautiful silver-white moonbeams pour in, giving us partial light as we quickly went off into dreams.

The next day standing around the luggage in the lobby, both of us quietly commented about the distance suddenly encountered around our "new friends" Eden, Maureen and Raymond. So, we cast it off as just a hiccup and started shuffling the bags into the bus taking us to the Puerto Vallarta airport customs area.

As we marched through the lines heading toward the departure area, our three new friends seemed to drift further and further away with each step toward the last gates and the planes. I offered to exchange cards and numbers, and Eden took mine with a "blank" quality in her facial expression and demeanor. The two other "new friends" seemed totally uninterested in any further contact, period.

All of this for some reason did not surprise Lora. In fact, she had told me earlier that it would all go down this way once we were close to departure. As we stood next to each other in the line, I commented to Lora as Raymond disappeared down another corridor with his bags, "Seems like one would call it an '*eight-day friendship.*' Eh?"

Lora gave me a condescending look and with a knowing kind of absolute in her voice said, "Didn't you understand that we were 'acceptable' play things for them only while they were here? … No other further contact was ever required."

"Hmm…odd, I imagined something different for a few odd moments and I'm still not sure you're totally correct."

"Well, I'm glad to get a *little* credit from you on this lovely day. Even if it's only a little."

Lora then turned and started pulling her bag slightly ahead of mine as we drifted down another slow moving narrow concrete corridor toward the boarding area near our plane.

During the actual flight to Seattle, Lora said little. She read three magazines and a small book instead. … Maybe two or three words we uttered between us. She seemed to have thrown a "shroud" on as a new cover and it was quite off-putting and cold. I thought she might have eaten a lot of ice before we left to get her to this level of "cold-disregard." A few other women I'd dated in the past could get into this obvious state of aloofness if they were "not pleased," and I guessed Lora was just another to add to the list.

At the Seattle airport, we just had our small bags and I suggested that we both celebrate the trip and return with a fine fish dinner at an airport branch of a restaurant with a fine reputation in the city. We had three hours to kill before our flight to Eugene. I thought we might talk and share some good wine and food prior to take off.

At dinner we shared light, superficial conversation about the immediate future and I offered to take Lora and her two grandchildren out for pizza locally. … She agreed to do that and asked me to call her regarding the actual date during the following week.

I was somewhat ill at ease with both her separation and coldness through dinner. I briefly brought up the subject of excess drink or over-smoking during the middle of the trip, but Lora seemed to completely deny what had happened. There was also no reference to her glaring fears of "abandonment" regarding me or all her past "troubles" during other periods of obvious intoxication.

"I think you are making far too much out of the incident, Robert."

"No. … I did see a very abandoned person — frightened as if she were center stage in an anti-religious cell block in Tehran prior to 'hard' questioning."

Lora pulled back immediately and denied all feelings regarding her state of mind…she was open about it…just to "get her position" out.

We finalized our positions and tried to smooth it all out with some fine Cabernet from eastern Washington. The wine was probably from the Walla Walla area and was one fine, drinkable bottle. As I paid the bill, Lora's look of both distance and damage remained stamped on her face. I tried to sublimate it and put it all somewhere else, but her expression and negated feelings, especially toward me, were troubling and remained pounding in my brain like a small tap hammer. Somehow in my gut I knew that there was little left for us — nothing in-between us… nothing in the future…nothing much at all.

For me the whole experience was one of "seeing" something deeply hidden in a person, a dark secret I should not have seen at all but did.

Lora could only run from me as she had from others so many times before because of the way she "viewed it." The many ways we see ourselves — what we imagine, both now and later —too often becomes an image we do not want to see of ourselves.

We never shared a dinner again, and the experience with her would remain in my head forever. ...It could be that the person I knew or *thought* I knew was never on the trip with me. Perhaps we were just strangers briefly brought together then never to view or exchange anything again...not even pizza.

THE PYTHON AND THE MONGOOSE

The Python & The Mongoose

⟨1⟩

In a very thick jungle south of Jaffna, Sri Lanka is a wild area that's fully protected by the government. For many years, countless animals, usually indigenous to India, have been "taken" — either smuggled or somehow traveled across — to the safety of the island's massive greenery. The Mongoose may have always been on the island, since it's natural also to India, yet other animals like the Python arrived another way. … These two animals from deep, epigenetic roots are and always have been natural enemies. … In a confrontation, the battle score is 50-50.

She was yellow, gray and blue-gold. Her scales reflected the embers of the sun's surface and yet she blended in perfectly with the jungle fauna. Her species had developed hunting skills over hundreds of thousands of years, perhaps millions of years, which made her one of the great predators in this dense terrain. Even the Cobra shied away from her, deciding to confront something else where the odds were in its favor. Fighting was not the Cobra's usual way, even though the Mongoose was an archenemy and confrontations and battles naturally occurred when they could not be avoided.

In this jungle domain, the Mongoose usually had triple the population numbers of the Python. Territories are far greater for the Python and its mates, and the Mongoose shares these same territories and tends to get along with its own kind. When the two animals came into the same area, most of the small animals and birds scrambled just to find "safe surroundings."

The usual time for the hunt is three in the afternoon, with both animals typically appear during this time. The mutual stalking begins separately. ... In some instances, these animals could attack the same prey at the same time; usually a small Guinea-rat that occupies this region in large numbers. This rat is a favorite treat for both animal, with the faster Mongoose usually catching double the number of the Python — sometimes even stealing the rodent right from the snake's "death squeeze."

⟨2⟩

Her name was Camille Longesse and she roamed the areas of the south and west from New Orleans to eastern Idaho — that was her territory. Usually she "manifested" herself as a psychic or a palm reader — illusive, yet attracting willing and entranced customers.

She'd always set her tent behind her van as she traveled through this "hard" country. She got to know one little town at a time, moving from one small place to the next. She was a true American beauty, maybe in her early 30s with black healthy hair and chiseled facial features. She had a low voice, green eyes and a smile that could easily take you in — man or woman. ... She was like a fantasy, the lovely-unquestionable witch in the mirror — a joyous, dark, longhaired beauty.

Her face was a cross of contemporary Pueblo Indian and deeply Spanish New Mexican with a slight touch of French Cajun. She was a perfectly shaped, solid package of sensual appeal that no man could take his eyes off of. ... She was a short-skirted beacon of desire lost in the open stars, a shining vision of an open *Roma* past and present.

She was a female feline seeking much more, and you could see it in her eyes. ... She was a woman few would not desire in some way. Yes,

Camille Longesse was a *gift* to all men who met her. Most felt nothing would be spared to obtain their prey. ... Yet the question could be posed: was she the prey or were they?

It was an amazingly clear 83-degree day in early spring, just outside the eastern part of Helena, Montana. Occasionally, Camille would team up with a carnival group, there were a few who knew her and delighted in her presence — especially when taking the 50 percent split of her "take." Many of the younger working cowboys, railroad men and construction crews would line up in front of Camille's tent. Most men just wanted to see her, be around her, smell her — the light sweet cologne evaporating off her sleek body and tanned skin was intoxicating. She always did well with the carnival and made more money than she usually did on her own, plus there was safety in numbers here.

⟨3⟩

It rained at the upper edge of the jungle canopy...the excess water dripping down on the large leaves growing on the excessive greenery and fauna below. As the light passed through the shadows, the Python moved far more quietly than expected — prey was near, and scent drove the large snake forward. At about the same time, the Mongoose was moving toward a medium-sized Guinea-rat from the opposite direction. ... The rat was not safe in any direction; its fate was surely sealed. ... Or was it?

The Python grabbed it with its sharp teeth, and began "gumming" it. The little rodent was in shock as the large predator quickly wrapped its powerful body around it in a powerful death squeeze. The rain began falling harder, and more and more water hit the ground. The sound was almost deafening. From a small shrub directly across from the Python, the Mongoose jumped upward, popping out of the bush. It hit the earth and startled the snake. It danced around the Python, which quickly envisioned a bigger meal and slowly began loosening its grip on the Guinea-rat.

The Mongoose darted and jerked in all directions…resembling the ethnic dance of festive peasant farmers celebrating spring. The dark eyes and large head of the Python could envision nothing but wrapping itself around the Mongoose…and so the Guinea-rat slipped away from the snake's clutches and to run into the shrub. The Mongoose faked in another direction and instantly grabbed the back leg of the Guinea-rat and gleefully pranced away with it in its mouth.

The Python begrudgingly watched the "winner" head off into the dense jungle. … Pleased with its victory, the Mongoose climbed into a safe tree and started devouring his prize. The Python would remember this incident, but accepted its loss but only for moment.

⟨4⟩

Antonio Stevens Gomez, an athletic man in his late 20s usually worked as a wrangler and artist for the U.S. Forest Service. He sauntered into Tiny Bronson's Carnival from the west gate, the one closest to Helena. Antonio was built like a super middleweight fighter — handling horses and mules all day helped, plus he usually kayaked a river section once or twice a week.

Antonio had graduated from the University of Montana in Missoula, and he and his kin were ranchers native to the region for the last hundred years. His background was sheep ranching via northwestern Montana, where the Basques settled in fair numbers at the turn of the 20th century. Antonio was an evolutionary biochemist, yet even with a Master's degree, work in his field was difficult to find. What he found most satisfactory was field work. He had a need to be "out there" alone in the back country wilderness — getting paid while working with animals was just a bonus. He was once engaged to a woman in White Horse, but that ended abruptly in a bout of jealousy over an ex-classmate and model he was close to. … He also had some other mildly sordid history.

As he paced through the carnival, he stopped to play a few games, challenged the wooded mallet bell ringing, and took a couple of rifle shots, winning a couple of minimum-sized Teddy bears, which he carried through the Midway of the small carnival.

As he turned the corner next to a large tent, he carried his yellow and bronze Teddy bears next to his chest. He spotted the van-tent and sign reading: "Camille, Psychic and Palm Reader." He thought, *Why not give her a little money and get a palm reading?* From the dust of the Midway path, he entered the tent behind a large man about the size of the center of a massive old oak tree. There was another man, probably a cowboy, in a black plaid shirt getting his reading. So the two of them waited their turns, one in front of the other. He could only see Camille's forehead and black bangs, but nothing else was visible as she concentrated on the cowboy's rough palm.

The man just in front of him was as large — about the largest man as Antonio had ever seen. In a way, he reminded him of a massive old bull buffalo arched on a low hill across in the eastern Montana prairie. Antonio was 6'2" with a sleek, muscular build. Antonio guessed he was a logger who gained all that muscle after years in horse and bull corrals across the upper ranch mountain regions of the state.

Antonio was a patient man, but the mystery of Camille's face stirred his instinctual curiosity and he desperately wanted to see more. The problem was the wide logger in front of him was an immovable object — no way could Antonio see around him.

Finally, the cowboy's palm reading was done, and the big logger moved up to quickly take his chair. Camille's dark green eyes and exquisite face glowed like they were lit from within by magic. She peered up directly at him as he shifted in his chair. He was immediately transfixed, almost lost in the cool green, lucid power emanating from her eyes. He thought, *I know in my heart this woman could be a tornado…but it would be worth trying.*

⟨5⟩

It started raining hard at the east end of the wild forest where the greenery was so thick that a large tribesman with a machete might fight to forge a path. … Yet it seemed a *dark beauty* surrounded this wild place. Once again out of nowhere the Mongoose moved quickly, darting from area to area looking for its next meal. At the center of this massive fog-filled jungle, the Python started slowly moving after being still for six days digesting his last kill. Renewed hunger droving him to move once again…and so everything in this large, intelligent snake awakened. At first, he appeared lethargic as he moved, but after working out the kinks in his muscles he started moving fairly rapidly. He seemed silent, but those that were aware enough knew he was on the move.

A baby monkey fell from the canopy above and thudded to the ground unconscious, not far from the sliding Python who seemed to reverse course instantly to move toward the sound. It all happened in seconds. Coming around dense fauna to the south of the noise, the Mongoose appeared instantly and appraised the situation like the ultimate prey-snatching, cunning animal it was.

The Mongoose quickly batted the Python's head with its claws and the large snake seemed stunned as it dropped the monkey's body. Quickly, its lower body and tail once again wrapped itself around the small creature, but the Mongoose stood its ground.

The decision facing the snake was to drop the small monkey and go for the larger Mongoose — a larger meal always enticed the snake. Or should he keep his current prize? The Mongoose jabbed its claws and teeth into the Python's upper body, forcing it to loosen its grip. Then, the Mongoose skillfully grabbed the monkey in its mouth and dashed into the encircling fauna.

After the loss, the Python moved upward to get a view above the bush and greenery. She watched the Mongoose escape with what had been her dinner. … Afterward, the large snake just stared into the dark bush for several seconds. It seemed to sense a deadly future encounter with the Mongoose — a fight to the death for one of them.

⟨6⟩

Antonio hardly spoke during his reading…and what a reading it was. The whole time, he couldn't take his eyes off her…no, not at all. Camille took everything in within her 'territory.' Her most clever skill was the ability to quickly and effectively glean an intimate understanding of her clients. She held Antonio's hand with a special guided softness reserved for her 'most favored' clients. Once a man entered "her tent," he was hers. She controlled his hand and a good deal of the emotional substrate above it. Men were "playthings" in her softness and easy touch. It was this way with nearly all of the men she encountered. Camille was a master diplomat, a conductor on an ever-present stage — the perfect master negotiator, especially when it involved something or someone she really desired.

After the palm/mind reading, Antonio felt like he'd just exited a Chinese opium den. His mind felt confused…foggy. He'd been somewhere else for a few seconds. It was like walking out of an intense hypnotic session. He could remember few of the words or thoughts he communicated during the reading with Camille. He did remember asking to share a drink with her at 8 p.m. at the well-known old-town country bar called Luke's Place. Antonio was mesmerized. He had met few women in his life as full of life and full of zest as Camille…few as sensuously alluring either.

At Luke's Place, they discussed the "world," and she listened attentively to almost everything he said. … She concentrated on him, giving him as much of her "all" as she could.

She entwined her fingers in the upper part of his hand…moving them in and out in a weaving pattern. At first, Antonio tried to move away to attempt "release" from her spell, but it was too late — he was gone. She took him like a spider lures her prey a web — the shining trap.

"How long are you going to be in Helena, Antonio?"

"Well originally I was planning on leaving tomorrow...but now I may stay a couple more days."

"Well...that might be a fine thing if you stayed...real fine."

Maybe it was the way she said it... it didn't really matter — he could spare a few more days. *Why not spend them with Camille?* he thought.

⟨7⟩

In a side cavern near the cave entrance, the Mongoose ate his small rodent. ... He took his time doing it...not as aware as usual of the sounds and areas around him. A heavy wind blew through the leaves, and there was a dense silence as the clever Python fell through the air toward a eucalyptus tree just beyond the big rocks between which the Mongoose was sitting. As the Mongoose gorged itself on the rodent's thigh, the Python dropped on him from above. Her muscular grip immediately started wrapping and tightening... and it continued.

At that moment a young Bengal Tiger came around the corner and leaped at the snake. In the ensuing chaos, her grip on the Mongoose relaxed as she tried escape disaster looming from hungry tiger. In the panic, the Mongoose scattered between the rocks and bush and quickly made its way into the forest. His leg was bleeding either from the tiger's swipe or the Python's teeth. The Mongoose somehow knew how close he'd come to a painful death courtesy of one of the two predators. ... He understood how aware he must remain at all times to keep his status from becoming 'prey.'

⟨8⟩

They soon made it to Antonio's lodge room at the western outskirts of Helena that night. His physical connection with Camille was beyond "lure" and far beyond the pull of her gentle psyche. The deep passion he felt was different from any woman he'd shared chance encounters or lovemaking with. He thought knew the difference between lovemaking and haphazard sex. A man's illusions can make their own reality sometimes, and then *absorbing dispersion....*

He held her hand all night, so close to her perfect naked beauty. ... It was all so overwhelming. ... She was more than any woman he'd *ever* known. He smiled to himself as he glanced at her sleeping. ... His body felt cold — a deep cold that remained — yet holding her in his arms was more important than sleep. ... *I'm so satisfied,* he thought.

He soon fell asleep, and as he did Camille arose and tenderly glanced at his relaxed muscular body, then she silently glided across the room toward the shower. She never liked the mixed sweat of an exhausted overheated body after sex and she needed "cleansing." In the shower she washed vigorously, soaping up everywhere, and scrubbing a little harder between her legs.

She meticulously worked the warm soap around her vagina and pressed inside using that pressure to "feel" clean. ... Using her fingers, she came close to pleasing herself again. ... She continued washing, to remove any possible remaining juices. ... She became less agitated as the task was completed, a warm shower after sex always did that for her and now she was more content.

She wiped the towel down her body, drying the beads of moisture as she went. Then she moved the towel to her black hair. Her clothes were on the back of the chair in this large bathroom, and she dressed quickly, then brushed her hair, finger cleaned her teeth with Antonio's toothpaste and quickly stepped through the door.

For a few seconds she stood there and watched him snoring and looking relaxed. She rapidly moved to Antonio's pants that were folded on a chair and took all the loose cash he had along with is Mastercard. She shoved the loot into her light colored jacket pocket, smiled to herself and left the room soundlessly. ... It was quite similar to a Red Fisher moving across the high mountain snow...a few light tracks and disappearance...only to appear another day.

⟨9⟩

The Python somehow escaped the young tiger's grip, but parts of her central torso were torn in the battle. She needed some rest and to heal, so she dragged her body into some deep, thick mud to stop the bleeding. After a few days of soaking in the viscous mud, she somehow knew she'd stopped bleeding and recovered. She could now return to the animal-filled forest floor and fill her belly with fresh prey.

The Mongoose roamed Mole-rat territory. Their warrens were usually tied together and hidden by small dried twigs. ... He finally found their home areas. Next to the Guinea-rat, the Mole-rat was his favorite food, although other rodents would do in a pinch. This most-desired prey was plentiful in the forest, though so he dined on his favorite often.

Before the kill and eating, for the Mongoose there was always the "play." So, rapidly the Mongoose tore into one of the many of the Mole-rat's hidden wooden hatches. The Mongoose was a clever hunter and always succeeded in uncovering good "healthy" prey.

⟨10⟩

A large line had formed in front of the entrance to Camille's tent. She always had customers — mostly men — and they paid very well for her services, sometimes as much as fifty or a hundred dollars including the tip. Suddenly, she spotted Antonio five bodies in back in the line. ... His face was distorted and angry, yet he waited patiently in line.

After an hour, Antonio was in front of her. He sat down automatically in the chair. She peered straight into his eyes, kept a "fix" on him, smiled, nodded, grabbed his palm and began her reading. At first Antonio said nothing and Camille seemed completely at ease, acting as if nothing had happened...nothing at all.

As she started reading his palm, she glided her touch, both tenderly and sensually dancing and shifting her soft fingers down his palm-lines.

This was crucial for deep palm reading, and is used by most higher end Big Top palm readers. It's a method rooted in gypsy culture for hundreds of years. These methods were skillfully used to start the "extraction" and set the *"mark"* up for "easy takings."

Camille was smart, beautiful and well spoken, along with being sexy, trained and creative — a perfect combo in the one-on-one carnival con game. She feared little and could play the *"mark"* perfectly, never diverting from the appearance of concern and truth. Antonio was taken in by her again, as if completely mesmerized by those dark green eyes and her sensual touch.

"You're bothered by someone, yet afraid to speak?"

"Yes, that is quite true."

"Wait four hours and meet at the lodge bar at 8 p.m. and your fear will evaporate."

"All right. … I can accept the meeting. I'll be there."

Camille squeezed his hand tenderly and Antonio stood to leave. She instantly grabbed the left hand of the next man in line behind him — another old cowboy in a worn checkered shirt. His hands were tough, worn and worked. She smiled gently at the old cowboy and it seemed like some of the deep lines in his face melted. Antonio slipped through the flaps in the tent's entrance and was gone.

⟨11⟩

The Python was hurt, yet recovering especially fast after devouring a large Mole-rat. The ongoing recovery had quickly taken most of the energy she'd gained by eating and it was time for the great snake to search for bigger prey. Its ancient genetics drew it again to the Mole-rat forage. It was unusual for the giant snake to return to prior feeding places, but those "twiggy" homes constructed for protection and camouflage were just too tempting to pass up.

Coming from another direction in the upper part of the forest the Mongoose darted in and out of the forest floor fauna. Immediately the he "caught" the change in the air and approached the mole-rat nests with some caution. … He'd scented a big predator close by, and extra caution was a smart move — and the Mongoose was nothing but smart.

Entering the Mole-rat area, the great snake naturally moved toward the newly completed Mole-rat burrows. …The area was surrounded by dense jungle and a few rock outcroppings — a perfect setting for a *blind* ambush.

The large predator quickly slid through the old abandoned burrows and found nothing. … So, she quickly moved to a dark stone ledge cutting through the inside of the burrow between the entrance door and the cavern within. … She lay there in wait for the next rat to enter. … Her black and deep green eyes glowed at bit in the dark with reflected light from the shelter entrance. The great snake seemed to smile ever so slightly as it coiled up in an "attack" position…waiting.

⟨12⟩

At about eight that evening, Antonio entered the door to the bar. In the corner, an old, dark, silver-haired woman *piano fingered* an old Sinatra song, cleverly skipping her chubby appendages across the keys — these were songs she'd played many times before. … Camille entered from another door to the bar & grille and sat right next to Antonio, who was sipping some bourbon whiskey at the long wooden bar. Camille ordered a French cordial and slid her fingers against Antonio's upper right hand. He keeps his fingers in place, tensing his muscles, even though the blood flowing through him seems to melt with her fine touch.

"So, you still play with the man you steal from, eh?"

"I've stolen nothing in life. … You pay for what you receive — sometimes with money and sometimes in other ways."

"Well, you sure look at life differently, my dear. So you're asking me to buy into your view?"

She slowly took a sip of her cordial and rubbed the additional liquid on her gums with her finger — lingering on the engrossing taste. "Buy into nothing, Antonio. If you were married or engaged or even dating — hey, you'd pay gladly. ... What's the difference? ... *What* is your issue?"

"You're just another carny-thief, the kind my old dad always warned me about."

"And you, dear child, *should be* warned. The carnival is a rough place — it's not for children. ... Let's move our discussion in another direction or I will be obliged to leave."

Agitated and not able to get his point across, a frustrated yet "interested" Antonio altered and quickly acknowledged Camille's request. "So, will you have dinner with me tonight...and will you stay with me?"

"Why not? ... But it will be dinner and $150 later for the reading."

"What reading? ... What reading did I have? ... When does it take place if I haven't had it?"

"I will do the reading with you in your room after dinner, then we move to the physical and emotional. ... Agreed?"

Antonio's hurt was deep. He was still attracted to her though, and there was nothing he could do about that. *She once again has a totally logical position,* he concedes, thinking liked a trained environmental scientist. "All right then, I'll accept your 'stuff' again, and I'll even go along with you not actually being a thief. ... Just a woman who's self-supporting, let's say?"

Camille smiled and pulled his hand over, palm-side up. She stares deeply into the lines, smiling like the Cheshire Cat, then she passionately kisses the back of his hand with full lips and a soft tongue, pressing tenderly.

"So, we understand each other now...don't we, Antonio?"

"I guess so. ... Yes, I guess so."

⟨13⟩

The Python silently rested at the jutting edge on the corner of the abandoned Mole-rat cave for many solemn hours — time had no meaning to the great reptile. Its major drives were always: food and survival, which for her meant being a predator.

Somewhere in the cave there are scurrying and nibbling sounds, and then the sound of clattering sticks outside the cave entrance. ... Something is entering quietly, and the Python's eyes slowly open. Two chocolate paws enter at first, then the animal's body shoots to the side of the cave, eyes aglow and checking for any sleeping Mole-rats.

Moving slowly and carefully, the Mongoose scans in all directions looking alert for both enemies and prey scents. As he looks above at the protruding portions of the cave's shelves, the Python curls up and instantly springs forward, landing atop the Mongoose. The "captured" Mongoose tries to flee the cave, pulling outward using its hind legs. The body of the snake wraps it up though, and the Mongoose can only move in limited directions. The snake pulls in, wrapping and tightening its upper body so the Mongoose is almost immobile. ... Then the great snake comes in for the final squeeze, draping its body over the completely over the Mongoose.

As it squeezes, bones begin to crack and then "breathing" slows...and finally there are no more sounds. In a few seconds, the Python releases the pressure and repositions itself to swallow the Mongoose whole. As it moves around, the "faking" Mongoose jerks up and jabs its formidable front claws into the Python's eyes and they bleed profusely, blinding the great reptile.

The Mongoose darts to another position near the Python's head, he then sinks his teeth into the reptile's left cranium, stabbing deeply into its skull. The sharp teeth penetrate the soft tissue around the Python's temple and the snake quickly curls and then unwinds as the Mongoose's sharp front fangs fatally wound its brain. The Python dies and slowly unwinds for the final time on the cave floor. The wise Mongoose holds its teeth in place until he's sure the Python is truly dead.

In battles with other snakes like the Cobra or King Cobra, the Mongoose is the winner only 50 percent of the time. Confrontations with snakes are rare, but when they come, there is no sure winner. It's usually a darting and twisting dance to the death with no *natural winner*.

⟨14⟩

After a sweaty and tossing lovemaking session, Antonio lay exhausted atop the white bed sheets. Camille opened her large green eyes and slid her perfectly proportioned lower torso from the queen-sized bed. ... It's a bright spring morning and a new dawn is breaking. Camille, moving like a Lynx, heads toward the large shower.

In the shower, she quickly soaps up and begins washing all the parts of her model-like body. As she washes, Antonio enters the shower and stands next to her in the fast-flowing water. He carefully and tenderly washes her large, reddened nipples and moves his fingers around her firm natural breasts. She is a woman who attracts him, and re-attracts him — and he doubts this attraction will ever end.

They make passionate and "close" love in the flowing shower water, and they climax at about the same time. When they finish, each exhausted from the interplay, Antonio starts to towel down as Camille finishes rinsing and turns the spraying water off.

"Do I owe you another $150 for that?"

"Of course. You know what the price is. There's always a price... always."

"Not this time. ... Let's call us even and move on. Okay?"

"No such thing as even — not even, not anything. You *will* pay what you owe."

"Or what? ... I will simply get dressed in the other room and leave, and I will leave owing you zero for any of it!"

"All right, Antonio. Do what you will, but remember there is always a price to be paid. Now or later — the price shall be paid."

"We'll see, my dear, we'll see. … I don't see life the way you do — I refuse to. … Life is not always *your way.*"

"It's always my way. When you play, it's always my way. … That is life and to get through it, to actually get through it…you and I must abide by the rules — either now or at another time."

Antonio smiled at her as he left the bathroom. Camille continued towel-drying her long hair and "heated" and dripping tanned body. Antonio got dressed and walked out to his waiting car, then drove off toward Sammy's Grill, a fine brunch and dinner place on the west side of Helena. After brunch he headed to the field office to finish some paperwork and to enter additional information in the climate computer system.

Antonio knows he'll head out for dinner… then eat, sleep and drive out to the western office in the early morning. The weatherman predicted clear and cold for the day. … Cold is something he knows well — he understands the cold.

After work, he decided to visit his hotel room, take a shower, and then head up to the Round-Up Grill for a large steak with all the trimmings — he needed some "real" food. He used his key to enter his motel room, which was dark as he slipped in. As soon as he closed the door and looked up, two huge, tough-looking carny men grabbed him. They punched him from both sides and he fell to the floor unconscious. … When he was down, they then took his wallet and all his cash and credit cards. One dumped a glass of water on his head, waking him, and then softly whispered in his right ear, "Next time you won't wake up! Don't call the cops, either. If that happens, we will track you down, 'pain you' and take your barely alive body to the far end of a mine shaft near here and drop it in. … Then we'll burn the remains. Do you hear me?"

"Yes, I hear you — no police…no nothing!"

"Good, we're just the 'collectors' nothing more. In the future, if I were you I'd always try to pay *what's owed*...might just save ya a little pain. ... Eh?"

His wallet fell near the side of his head. His face hurt. *Maybe a broken facial bone or two,* he thought. His ribs smarted too — possibly deeply bruised he guessed. Suddenly he heard Camille whisper as he writhed in continuous shooting rib-cage pain. "In the dance of life, there's always an *exchange* and one shall *always* pay what's owed...someday."

From the corner of his swelling and blackened eye he saw her red skirt, shapely legs and high heels pass by him and leave through the door, shutting it behind her. Soon he heard the familiar sound of a diesel Ford truck power down the road.

THE RENEGADE AND THE GUNRUNNER

CIRCA 1862

The Renegade and The Gunrunner

CIRCA 1862

Jim Corbett

My cousin Jim Corbett and I grew up in Southern Illinois, Kentucky and Southeast Missouri, sometimes on and sometimes near the Mississippi River. His father, Will, and my Uncle Kane were blood brothers, with two sisters they shared, May Jean and Katy Lee, my favorite aunts. Jim's father, Kane, was a bargeman and at the time had about three fellows working for him in his company. They worked together along the Ohio River near Paducah, Kentucky.

Uncle Kane was a large man, about 6'2", and weighed 'round 240. He was a strong man and as hard a worker as you could find. He had a "heart" for his men and was 'bout as loyal as one could fine. When you worked for Kane Corbett, you and your family were set — he loved a man with a solid family behind him.

At times Jim and I worked hard for his dad in the late '50s. Both of us were 'bout the same age and size — 'round sixteen as I remember. .. Kane instructed Jim on all aspects of barge and hauling. At first, Jim took it all "light" but after a while it all began to seep into his head, and some of that stuff ended up stickin' in my head too...yes, indeed.

111

Jim's sister, Katy Lee, was one buxom woman in her early 20s. She seemed to work right along with her brother Kane, yet she specialized in keeping the books and contracts — she was always the smartest cookie around in either of the clans. Kane trusted Katy Lee beyond all others. Sometimes I thought Jim's mom was just a pinch jealous of this, especially 'cause Katy Lee was also a fine dancer — she could really dance! She could drink *and* dance most men way under the table, plus she could usually out think 'em too. She was one hell of an aunt!

Rene Corbett ~ The Renegade

In those days, during the late 1850s, the family was solid — we were all were real close. The war a few years later would change that forever. My name is Rene Corbett, most call me Cousin Rene the "renegade." They refer to me that way 'cause I never wanted to do anything under orders — never believed in bein' told what to do. … Was always hard for me to fathom obeyin' 'em, even as a kid, yes indeed. Later in my life some of that would change, as it does as life moves on.

My dad, Will, and our family lived near Cape Girardeau on the Illinois side of the Mississippi River. My dad and mom owed a large grain farm near Jonesboro, a good farming area just north of Cape Girardeau. Even in those days my dad was considered a real smart one, so he quietly sent me to college in Carbondale. … The little college specialized in agriculture, animals and grains…so, off I went in '58.

I always kept real close to Jim Corbett, he was more like a brother to me than a cousin, since I was cursed with sisters and no brothers. My dad and mom had three girls — one died of croup at age three. My two sisters were Beth Nicole and Kendra. Both married off early to some farmer's sons in northeast grain country. My sisters and I were never close anyway, and after the marriages we seldom saw each other —they had families of their own to tend to. That was okay 'cause Jim and I always remained close in those days.

Uncle Kane and his family worked hard to develop a growing shipping and hauling business. Yep, he always seemed to keep buying more haulers, barges and other equipment for shipping. He also bought two other companies out before they lost everything. Uncle Kane's company was growing fast.

When I came back from Carbondale College in late 1860, my Uncle Kane had become a shipping magnate — a major player along the rivers. Now it has to be said that Jim worked real hard himself and got to know the business on the outside as well as Katy Lee had on the inside. On the rivers, he was almost as knowledgeable as Uncle Kane. No matter where Jim was, he always dressed well, and outside of business he always wore the best of St. Louis shop clothing. He was an up and coming businessman and the son of a successful businessman.

When we were kids Jim was always a tough one — he knew how to use his fists. He was well trained by a tough man on the docks named Josh Steel, who was an ex-professional knuckle boxer and street fighter in his early days. Even at the near 40, Josh Steel could take down nearly any man, no matter his size or power. Jim learned fighting well from old Josh, and Uncle Kane seemed proud of the way Jim practiced and kept himself trained and at the "top of his boxing game."

I remember I was with both Josh and Jim in a rowdy bar on the northern side of the Ohio River in a small barge town called Metropolis. There were all kinds of bargemen there along with others who worked ten-twelve hours a day on the docks...and there were always a couple of large freemen sitting in a corner deemed acceptable for local working blacks.

This strapping fellow, an extremely large man, came in. I believe he was from Caruthersville, in north Kentucky along that part of the Mississippi. He was named Blythe Williams, and he had a reputation for 'nasty' as big as he was — and that was over 250 pounds of molded muscle. Josh, Jim and I were at the bar near the middle when Blythe just came over and moved Josh and Jim so he could sit in-between — a somewhat discourteous move, one could say.

It all started with some harsh table talk about a dark haired bar girl Blythe had a 'grin on' for. ... Whether their relationship was real or not, *she was his!* ... Josh just had to comment, and that got it all going...yes, it did!

"So, you like that dark haired little filly, do ya?"

"Yeah, she's with me, if you really want to know. ... But it makes no difference to me either way...'cause I can see your eyes on her — and that's not good!"

Josh had the experience of men wanting to fight him in one bar or another along the Ohio all the time, and he knew exactly (to the second) where a conversation was going. ... This one "was going," he commented later. "Yes," he said, "they always go the same way...*sideways!* It's never a surprise."

As fast as anyone could move, maybe faster, Jim and I watched Josh hit this big man squarely in the nose. I could swear that I heard something crack then...and this really large burly bargeman went down instantly in free fall. He hit the dirt floor with a potato sack-like thud! He just laid there on the floor and didn't get up. Finally, four other large men carried his body to the back of the bar.

"Never saw a man go down like that...*never,*" Jim said.

"When a man's ready to pound you without notice...and you get that feeling that he's just about to strike...you swing first — hard and straight ...no point in waiting."

Jim Corbett learned a great deal from Josh, about boxing but mostly about thinking. Later when calls for the war came, that kind of learning and smarts would save his life.

Josh always thought he was one step ahead of most of the men he'd known. His mind just seemed to be trained that way. Of course, Jim said he learned from Josh mostly through experience, like watching and anticipating the Blythe Williams incident. That showed Jim intelligence and experience at their best.

There were many tough bars, and many hard places where the bargemen gathered along the Ohio and Tennessee Rivers. ... These were the watery areas and small towns meandering along the way to the old Mississippi. In those many months Josh, Jim and I would work with the bargemen in those areas. Jim and I were "allowed" to play because of Uncle Kane and his growing shipping and hauling business. It was expanding throughout the whole Girardeau Basin area, and along the Ohio River and all 'round Paducah.

One day, Josh and Cousin Jim got hold of me, and asked if I'd ride over with them 'bout 65 miles west to Poplar Bluff, Missouri — a wild mixed breed, gun running town in Southeast Missouri. One of the main trading posts there was called Patty's Goods and Guns. In fact it was a gun running barter post used by both legal and illegal runners to supply fur traders, mixed breeds, and other shadow groups with all kinds of up to date tradable weaponry.

I agreed to accompany Jim and Josh on a Saturday when none of us was formally working at anything. The infamous old man called Gordon "Hard Tack" Leeks owned and ran Patty's Goods and Guns. He agreed to visit with Cousin Jim…about something…or some kind of business that his dad was directly involved in.

The trip took us about three hard-riding hours as we trotted along at a steady pace. We rode along Route 60, and on the way we saw goods of all sorts headed in and out, some towards the east and others going south towards the port of Charleston along the mid-southern Mississippi. It was late1860, and I remember lots of heavy oxen driven carts haul- ing eight wagons, movin' 'em along the road from Poplar Bluff east. … They all just kept moving, hauling right along down the tough muddy track. … There was lots of cartage along that road for sure.

As we got closer to Poplar Bluff, one of the many open wagons broke down and rolled over, spilling its contents on the side of the road…along with the heavy canvass top that usually hid and protected the load. The wagon was filled with bright, newly polished silver Sharpe Carbines — all spanking new. They spilled over and were just a gleaming at us in the midday sun… dropped right there at the side of the road.

"What ya think of that wagon, Jim?"

"Just some clever guy making some good money off those new carbines I'd say," Josh replied.

Josh rarely ever mentioned money or much of anything, yet there sure was a glint in his eyes looking at those spilled silver carbines.

"Josh, why don't you take some of that boxing prize money you won at Paducah and buy you one of those beautiful carbines?" Jim asked.

"Maybe 'cause I got too many of those little ones to feed…which is not a problem for either of you young playboys. … Eh?"

I thought about what Josh said, and it didn't really perturb me until much later — maybe a couple of years later, 'round the year when the War Between the States started 'tween North and South. Thoughts like that are carried with you, deep within you, and during troubled times can suddenly surface. Who knows what brings those memories out like word dreams. No one knows, but they do come.

Once we got to Poplar Bluff we made our way to Lee's Bar & Dance Hall, a place with a local reputation for wayward women who brought all kinds of "special games to the party," according to Josh.

"Let's all have a cold drink back at Lee's after our business with Mr. 'Hard Tack.'"

"Not such a bad idea, Josh. I like it. That's what we're *maybe* going to do. … I'll get us a hotel room too. … I think we'll take care of that trading business tomorrow after a drink or two. … A hard ride, and we'll be ready for 'Hard Tack' early. Papa Kane's given me the money to do all of it. … Be a good trip, indeed!"

"Well let's have a little fun, Jimmy-boy before you, Rene and me got to get down to business with old 'Hard Tack.'"

"Sounds like a fine idea. Maybe we can adjust the meeting for the morning. … Getting a little late now, eh, Rene?"

"I guess so, but I know Uncle Kane sure wanted us to meet with him today, not tomorrow…sure know that."

"My guess, Cousin, is we'll all be 'fresher' tomorrow. … Yeah, a drink or three, a little dancing and such…then a good solid sleep followed by business in the morning. … Yes, I vote for that!"

"And I second that," said Josh.

That night was the wildest one I'd had in my almost 20 years. We kept going hard until about three in the morning — drinking, dancing and bedding a few of the local fillies. … Didn't learn much that night but had a great time—we all did.

The morning light came up hard, particularly upon Jim and me 'cause we knew we had to get ready real soon for Mr. Hard Tack. Uncle Kane had some hard numbers Jim and I had to deal with for that meeting. The meeting took place in the corner of Mr. Leeks' bar. The whole facility seemed really quiet so late in the morning.

I remember old Hard Tack just sitting there, cold-faced and steady as Jimmy presented our deal —900 rifles, 20 carts, and various wheat products to be supplied to the shipping company for around $5,000 a month on a continuous basis. Kane's business had grown large in recent years and he was big enough to make that kind of deal.

"Your company can sell all that stuff in a month, Mr. Leeks?"

"We can, sometimes sell more. When the war breaks out, you'll our orders triple."

Mr. Leeks looked across at us in a piercing discerning manner, at all three of us including Josh…then he asked a few more penetrating questions. "What side your daddy be on when the war breaks out, Jim? It will break out…and soon."

Jim smiled, drank some of his beer, put two fists on the table and said, "The South of course, sir!"

Old Hard Tack Leeks just grinned, put his hand out to shake with Jim's and then looked at the two of us and said, "Be no deal at all if you'd mentioned another direction!"

We all cracked a grin and drank our beers as Jim handed Mr. Leeks $7,000 U.S. dollars, which he counted quickly.

"We'd like to take the carbines back today in three wagons to seal the deal. … That all right with you?"

"Well that will work, plus we'll give you three good haul wagons to seal the deal. That'll get you back there with the goods!"

"Yes sir, that'll close the deal all right."

Jim said little as we rode back to Paducah. He just sat high and hard in the saddle like any other young and proud Southern man, knowing full well that Uncle Kane would be proud of the fine and lucrative arrangement he'd made with the old trader.

Later, Jim and Uncle Kane would make many a deal with that trader and others around Missouri, Kentucky, Tennessee and Illinois — from Springfield to Charleston, including many other merchant bays around the Ohio and Tennessee rivers. The barge and shipping cart business was really growing and *war* could expand it ever more. ... There was always a "game" to play because business surely was a set of games, manipulations and vast compromises.

Next thing I remember I was in our family house near the old Mississippi, still in Illinois, when news of the war broke out in early 1861. ... Weren't much of a surprise, we all knew it'd be coming at us. My dad declared himself and his crops for the North, and I had to go along with him. ... His brother Kane and everyone in his family would be disappointed, though most knew what Dad's loyalties were and how he'd go.

So, as it went the big grain farm and all of us supported the North and that was the general direction for most folks in the Cape Girardeau area...it was Illinois, yes, it was *still* Illinois — home to Mr. Lincoln. My dad said that he had news that Uncle Kane and the rest of his family were going in the other direction and yet as family we were still invited to Jim's wedding to Mary Kathleen Lawrence.

She was a fine lady from a great Southern family living down-river near Mayfield, Kentucky. It was said they had a large plantation with many crops, and about 60 slaves. A great number of freemen and whites also worked for them, all the way down to Humboldt, Tennessee. Living down there was both wild and sparse, yet you could grow nearly any crops in that good soil. They chose mostly soy, sorghum and corn.

Later during the war, the Lawrence family would grow rich supplying both sides (for a while) with corn. … They'd have especially valuable contracts with the Northern army after a loyalty contract was signed when the army took the area. Even post contract signing Mr. Lawrence still played both sides of the food supply game. As the dark war went on, his pockets near exploded with wealth and his family never really suffered as others did from the intensity of the war. Sadly he did lose his second oldest son, William, at Gettysburg.

Jim and Mary's wedding at Mayfield Farms was one *huge* event, with all kinds of servants, many guests, great food and drink, and a good ole Southern band to dance to, naturally. In fact, they even got a "local truce" called for the wedding in "kindly spirit" honoring the two fine families merging into one massive commercial clan.

Uncle Kane was dressed in a well-tailored gray suit, and my Aunt Gilda Anne looked so lovely in her fine pink and blue dress with a large bonnet. They both certainly dressed perfectly well for the occasion. Cousin Kayla and her younger sister, Darla, were drinking quality sparkling wine like there was no tomorrow. … Fact was, Kayla even danced with Josh, and said she always liked a man with muscles. As they danced around, she never was shy about letting him know it…never shy. Yes, sure was a lot of solid folk kinda swinging and swaying all round, sure was.

Jim seemed to enjoy himself drinking and a dancing with Mary Kathleen, and yapping with his friends. Yet all around us, the *dark specter of war was certainly in the air*. Later that night, Jim, Josh, I, along with a couple of Jim's friends sat out on the great Lawrence porch talking away about the present and the future. … It was *different* for all of us, and the lively conversation was far deeper than most 'usual' kinds of words. What was said would be remembered long after the food and drink wore off…discussion centered on *our place* in the war.

Sometimes when it was just the right temperature during the fall (it was late October 1861), the fog just seemed to slowly drift in from the lower valleys and Reelfoot Lake. … That cold, dark fog just creeps in like fierce ghosts leftover from late the summer dew. ... The whole area had odd weather patterns — storms, fogs and floods. ... Always had 'em since I could remember.

We all just sat on that grand porch like older, contented men, spinning tales, smoking some fine Kentucky cigars and drinking aged Kentucky bourbon...near as smooth as brandy. Sure was a grand old wedding... was a *fine one*. ... One to be remembered.

"So, you're going in, eh, Rene? You joining up be part of the 13 states in the fight?"

"No, Jim, haven't given a thought to joining up or nothin' like that. ... Just continuing to help Dad with the farming business. ... Guess that's my short-term view."

"Not getting married like me? Just remain a renegade all your life, eh? Army of the South could really use a man that thinks an' shoots like you, Cousin. ... Could even lead a couple of humble men, I'd guess."

"Could do that, maybe. ... Right now, I got no plans to join up, just a keep workin' on farm business with your Uncle Will."

Jim and Josh kept silent for several long seconds — might have been longer, maybe a minute or two. Their eyes and facial expressions said it all.

"Well then, I'll be in the 21st Kentucky Regulars, yes I will. Mostly be doin' all I can to save the homeland from all those giant merchant bastards from the North. ... Brothers apart are never really brothers anyway."

"You sure beat up a few of them in the past, Josh. Especially during those days working the docks in New Orleans, eh?"

"Sure did, Jimmy. Guess now I'll just have to aim better and end the old way of life by a' battlin' an' killin' those *nigger loving* bastards."

I rose to my feet, lifted my drink and toasted Jim and Josh. It was in those early months of the coming 'good war' and we were all optimistic.

"Old Bourbon and smoke, always a great way to share the future with brothers. ... Cheers!"

Jim ended up in the 1st Kentucky Calvary as a Captain — nothing that boy couldn't do! ... He was always a natural leader and the commanders could see that. ... After training, he headed off to Chattanooga where a major clash was brewing.

At that battle, Jim lost most of the use of his left shoulder and lower left arm. ... He was also wounded by metal shrapnel. ... After the hospital, Jim just went right back to the river barge business, soon after the battle. ... He was lucky to be slightly wounded and end up "nearly whole."

Josh fought bravely in a large battle near Memphis. In fact, he fought in several defensive battles protecting that great city. Ended up losing his right arm to a split cannon ball, yet it didn't kill him. Sure did affect his attitude though. He wasn't a full boxer any more and ended up back in the barge business working for my Uncle Kane and Jim. He worked the docks anywhere along the Ohio, and even with one arm he still beat many a man in a few grungy bars along the river. ... Except for the arm, he seemed to change very little...yet there was a *difference* in him. I noticed it soon after he returned from battle.

A year from the start of the war, I joined the 22nd Illinois Artillery as a First Lieutenant. I was called in to help General Grant in the assault on Memphis. ... It was a terribly long and savage battle that never seemed to end. Many times we had to bombard gun emplacements for days, 'til we ran out of shells and had to retreat until we could re-supply. I eventually became somewhat deaf from being so close to all that shelling. No side really won the battle, but after six months of siege the Grand Old Union Army took the city with a lot of bloodshed.

We moved on to Vicksburg and another horrible siege and large loss of life. ... Many men and a massive number of civilians died there or came out short a limb or two. Supplies were always iffy, yet I can remember eating canned corn and I do remember reading the label that said, "Grown in Cape Girardeau, Illinois." ... Was always proud of my father, Will, for doing what he did — farm and farm well...and supply the Union troops without gouging the army.

The blood and dismemberment did more to change me than any flesh wounds I'd received in the war. ... These terrible wounds of war hit our area pretty hard — half the men I'd known had either been killed outright or wounded pretty badly. Many of those wounds were deep, very deep, if not directly crippling.

There was no glamor in the war on any side...too many men were killed or horribly wounded. Hate brings that on, puts a hard crust on already dried and rough wounds. There were hard times after the war. commerce and farming slowed at least for a few years. In later years, I became a land lawyer and worked for a good-sized firm in St. Louis.

Uncle Kane, Jenny Lee, Jim and Kayla sold most of the barge business, just kept a branch to work with in the future. Tools, iron and steel held, and they kept the best moneymaking parts of the business and resettled in Carbondale. The family was pretty well known there and had a good reputation for solid business practices.

I married a woman named Julie Adams Cromwell from a well-known investment and banking family in the St. Louis community. We were quite happy in our courtship and marriage and had three fine children — Tim, Louise and Tracy. We were all still quite close, as most of Corbett family was, yet we hadn't seen Uncle Kane and a good deal of the rest of the family including Jim much for the last ten years.

One day, we received a letter from Jim's fine wife asking us to all come down to Carbondale and spend some time with the family after Uncle Kane's funeral. I was truly saddened by the accident that killed good ole Uncle Kane. He was one tough old guy, but too many years of barging and stress had gotten to him and he didn't see the loose crane flying overhead. A large piece of industrial tooling broke from it and smashed him on the right side of the head. It cracked his shoulder and skull. It hit him so hard it just flipped him over, one of the workers had reported to Jim. … Uncle Kane was dead pretty much on impact.

I loved Jim's new wife, she was 'bout the best fast dancer I'd ever met. Jim wasn't a bad dancer either, but nothing like his wife...exciting. His wife's family, the Crowley's, were prosperous millers from Mayfield, Kentucky. They made a lot of money, but Mr. Crowley had died during the war. They had done well as a mid-sized war business…lots of good solid local businesses got rich during the four years of the war.

My dad danced with Jillian and her sisters, Rose Lee and Tammy Lora, and drank and had a real good time at Jim and Jillian's wedding… that was a fact. … Old wound and a little pain came from a small caliber bullet piece sunk in my left buttock that buried itself there during the siege of Memphis. A minor injury compared to most…just minor.

Near the end of the wedding I had a chance to talk to Little Wil (an old friend of Jim's), Jim himself and Cousin Abel and Beau from Malden, Missouri. The boys ran a little horse ranch in the southeast area. … They sold a grand number of horses during the war…hell of a lot of good horses…sure did. … Traded a few slaves, too…according to Jim.

"Old Uncle Kane would have enjoyed your wedding, Jim."

"Yes, he would have, Abel, but I guess the good Lord just wanted to take him…so there he must be."

"Well, I'd say old Uncle Kane was a brick-stubborn man sometimes, but our whole family really loved him. … He helped us transport our horses and *Niggers* down river through many parts of the Tennessee many a time during the war…at no cost sometimes, too."

"Yeah, old Uncle Kane helped many a man…always there to help. … He was one of those who could wait for his money…never pressed ye… never."

"My dad always loved your dad. There was something special about their brotherhood…kind of *made* the person…maybe even a son proud of being around them. … You support that, Rene?"

"Yeah…met a couple of brothers like that during the war. … In fact, when we fought at Bull Run, Craig and Peter Wallace — they really were a great example of brotherhood. They married women who were friends from the time they were *young-uns*. Sadly, Peter was hit by a large piece of cannon fodder and died instantly — a good part of his skull was blown out."

"Tough war on both sides, Cousin. … Glad all of us can stand here and talk about it. … Talk about it with our cousins Abel and Beau…yes, indeed."

"You know if Rene here wasn't a first cousin and growed-up with us, I don't think I'd be able to talk to another Yank…war kinda soured me on all Yanks. … Maybe I killed too many of them and all that blood kind a made me darker."

"You always had a lot of anger in you, Abel, even as a kid. … Sure remember that. … You and Beau was always a close part of the clan, so many feelings still remain connected to 'family'…. Maybe it's better not to discuss hate and who's a brother or not. … Maybe this soon after the war…we all got some hurt and we got to deal with it."

Jim looked at Rene after he spoke and knew he was exactly right about all the wounds the war caused on all sides, so many brothers and their *honorable* wounds, mortality and hate all mixed up together in their thinking. … It was a real hard time for all who fought in all those battles, skirmishes and combats during those four years of slaughter.

"Maybe a war kills off some part of each of us. Again, maybe it's just too much to discuss so soon after the battles…remember it's only 1866. Just a year after the war's end. … So, cousins, let's just share some of that fine Kentucky whiskey and enjoy the wedding festivities. What do you say?"

All the men were silent for several seconds. All of them except Rene had been wounded physically, each carrying "some of this war" as a visible mantel and reminder of direct combat. The suppressed trauma that did lay deep within all the men who served and fought was less visible, but possible more damaging.

Beau got out his granddad's fiddle and played a fast 'jig and reel' and Jimmy got up and started dancing hard with his sister. She just grabbed him, twisting him 'round and moving with that fiddle music. *Yes, sir,* they danced like two trained for the perfect 'reel.'

After the wedding I didn't see Cousin Jim for at least six months. One day, I rode down to Uncle Kane's barge company to visit with him, and maybe go out and share a lunch and a beer. I wanted to just talk some like we did when we were younger. When I came through the office door, his clerk asked me what I wanted …and I told her who I was. I asked her to tell her boss I'd like to see him. She told me he was just about through with an important meeting and would soon be out.

When Jim entered the room, he was obviously overjoyed to see me. He was using a cane now, and later told me that the other bullet stuck in his hip was currently bothering him causing him some "walking trou-bles." We hugged each other with the usual family warmth, then he asked if I'd ate yet, and I quickly said no.

"Well, brother, then let's you and me go down to Juliette Cagan's Restaurant and eat some fine crab and gumbo. … You'll surely love her gumbo…like the kind they serve in New Orleans I've been told."

We walked to the restaurant talking of family, good local wine, cur-rent events, women, and of course business along the rivers. This was always a topic of conversation.

When we sat down at our table, Jim ordered a bottle of fine French wine plus the appetizer of the day, some soft French cheese delight that came with homemade wheat crackers…all of it was real quality.

"Well, Rene, big farming business still good up there on the old river?"

"Well, it's good, brother, but I'm feeling a little 'creaky'. … Kinda anx-ious 'bout movin' somewhere different. … Need adventure, though. … Maybe a new life, eh?"

"War wasn't enough adventure for ye? … Me? I'm more than happy where I am. … Got a great Southern woman and a kid coming. … She thinks it's a boy…we'll see…and business is booming way beyond what Papa Kane did. … Whole river and rail system's *really* growin' now."

"For me, it's time for something new, maybe different — something I'm just not gettin' 'round here. So, we'll be heading west to California. … Got a little opportunity near Sacramento through a few solid contacts. Got a good-looking investment deal in some feed lots in the county, too, and I know that business…that I do!"

"You do. ... Yet, I thought you'd most likely be 'going into' the gold business there like a few others gone that way. ... You're headed somewhere in the same direction."

"No...never saw mining gold as easy in any way, plus, Dad always said, 'Do what you know best, you can't miss if you know the business!'... Plus, I've always wanted to write, develop *something* of my own with my good wife. ... So, I'm saying goodbye, brother."

A small tear appeared on the left side of Jim's face. He seemed struck by this news, struck harder than even he understood. It was like some replay of the emotion from the war years, and all kinds of memories and sounds just a kept popping into his head.

"Well, Cousin, or should I say Brother, since that's what you always were to me. ... Love ye, Rene, boy...and I'll miss you real deep. ... Hope you return soon, even if it's only for a visit."

"Won't be real soon, I can tell you that, Jim. Of course Mom's here and my lovely sisters, and you and the rest of the family, so naturally we'll be back within the next few years I'd expect."

There was silence for a while as Jim wiped his eyes with a large yellow handkerchief. Then he lifted his wine glass to Rene and toasted quite openly, "To the family, brother, to the great family Corbett!"

"Yes...to the great family Corbett!"

The food came as they each re-framed the next of their words, quite unsure of what to say or how to say it.

Rene only returned to the area once, when his mother died some years later. That was the last time he could "cling" to the warmth of his whole family. ... All of 'em were so deeply scarred by the war. yet no one could really talk about all the many marks and wounds it left on them... *never.*

~ END ~

Poetry Collection

The Artist

The artist stroked the sides of the granite walls…
chalk, stone and fingers plotted his inner drive…
colors *taken* from the earth's bounty….

Knowing the dark and fearful nature of the cave,
he plotted on, he drew the figures he knew, with materials he
understood, he was a *master* of colors, changing surfaces and
display.

The winds blew through the long cold tunnels
and out-corners of the cave's 'hidden places'…
yet an 'eeriness' remained in the whistling sounds,
as they cut their roaring echoes deep within…

And then the torches burned wildly,
held up by two sons, and a younger brother…
for they knew the power of his 'sacred' designs.

He scraped surface and pounded rough space…
so, all was prepared for the curves of mighty creatures
splayed on the cave's inner surfaces….

There were orange, red and silver images of hunts and gatherings
deeply imbedded in the hearts of his people. Dances, celebrations and
births, predator and prey depicted in outcrops, drawings and designs
using his skilled hands…for he was an 'artist' without name, a member
of a human tribe dwelling in dark caves so many thousands of years earlier bringing 'humans' something beautiful and essential to 'grow' our
layers… small spaces collectively shared in our imaginations and cul-
tural remembrance. …

He grasped and pulled **forces** from the cave's mantel…as drawings conjoined. …

So… as the torch fires burned down and smoldered…the discoveries came brilliantly…and are not these many inner images imprinted within 'all' in shadow areas of 'a collective consciousness?'

And when the 'artist' passed, his impressions on rock walls remained…continuing the never-ending tune of life that all 'true' artists lay at our feet to imbibe and cherish. …

*As it continues,

Steve Dreben, 11/23/14

White Light

From its massive burning galactic surface…
Intense images of a flashing star
Reminds us of the intense power of 'light'. …

And I but a soldier in a distant camp wait through the
centuries for **relief**…yet the 'light' seems out there. …

So, it spreads its warm essence through my soul
and it heats me in the bitter winter…
Gales and snow-driven ice pummel me in their
crystal <u>whiteness</u>… and I only a soldier in a distant place. …

As reflected on the sun's scorching surface glowing white-light separates
between dark spaces and pure clarity…. Unaware we are blessed to dance
in-between…in-between the spaces…and so we separate, yet ironically
share this 'wondrous' glow.

A 'babe' erupts in oxygenated blood from the dark of a mother's womb…
light reflects again coming to 'soak' L'Enfant in its living embrace.

Then the night comes and the soldier waits for early dawn…
and hopes that it 'shares' its force …yet another time.

And so 'life' itself becomes a chariot of **bursting light** which
absorbs all in *'a fire' for living…*

S.R. Dreben, 12/28/14

Transcendence

Breath is hard, wounded gasping lungs…
unable to accept proper allotments of precious oxygen…

A nobility of form reaching upward, stretching arms above…
finding a majesty in the blinding spaces between distant stars…

A contentious fight between form and non-form…programmed
chromosomes battling to remain…and yet there is a *magnificence*
that draws…pulls towards *the great source.*…

When night comes, energy drains like great batteries losing
alchemical power…

A magic emerges in the chaos…nothing that seems to be
what it is…is there anymore…

A slow transcendence <u>emerges</u>
…and life mixes with its 'deeper sources'… and peace comes…
a peace like no other.…

And she walks the dark corridors smiling and crying,
for then 'a magnificence' of human transcendence can
once again have short joyous consciousness…and again so quickly
memory fades…

Oh, lovely life…played once again so fully…so joyfully.…

S.R. Dreben 5/25/14 "Ode to a soul".…

Meditation

Contemplation of living forces…
Sitting still…sitting very still…eyes shut….
Flow…the continuous magic of creation…
like tumbling river currents crashing on rocks in fall…
such sound and power for a short time….

Deepened moments of connection, of balance…
of reflection…centered reflections…
sometimes finding snapshots of peace….

Ah, slowing the mind clock, our bio-rhythm…
slowing it towards a more tranquil pace…
I hear sounds, glimpses of inner balance of places 'reached for'…
crying out, crying for stability…better…deeper continuity…
some inner symmetry.

And so, the 'flow' continues…as once again 'it' may be achieved.
Breathing is paced and perfect, no smoke neither in nor out…
"A clarity" is found somewhere near the canopy of ancient trees…
moving in gusts….
And breezes blow, tides rise and fall and the 'turning' continues
inside…outside….

Finally, it slows and no masks are visible, <u>breathing the only sound</u>….
Rhythms of winds and bodies mix…
a matching of inner and outer concoction…but for a short period…
And we waltz off prancing with the stars just for a while….

S.R. Dreben, 4/13/14

Renewal~Rejuvenation

Boots crush the crystalline snow...
Early morning's frozen forms...
Following steep paths of winter
Across blizzard strewn and windy mountain trails....

Ascending instinctively through 'blurs' of time...
A slow beating rhythm of life renews itself beneath
crystal ice and frozen spaces....

Rhythms of life reawaken for Spring's displacement; and the
force of continuous rejuvenation once again appears...
first in tiny green shoots in spattered patches of mountain meadows...

And then a consummate crescendo of life pours forth through a post
frozen hibernation...and the surging energy of life buds forth...as the
sounds of babes cry out...waiting for spring's nurturing...which brings
yet another surge...YES!

And we hold hands dancing on the *green*…
We hold loving caress for life's beginnings…
part of *'eternal'* spring which opens hearts
to its consuming flowing powers….

The Alchemy of life is ours…and the Spring holds a glory
of that living force in *its all*…whole energizing hands….

Spring's rejuvenation…a continuous pounding flow of life *swirling*…
blown winter's snows atop a sacred and hidden mountain meadow….
Lucky are we who *are* part of this miraculous power…a power of nature's
continuous fulfilling grace….

"I shall inhale you inside me yet one more time…."
(Epigenetic Nature)

S.R. Dreben, 1/25/14

Magnificence of Ecstasy

Our beings *energize* with power…
as we continually search for acknowledgment, recognition…
and yet '*it* 'envelops us….

For a living blindness contains us…
dwelling too long in the non-living…
scratching chalk-board surfaces for 'sounds!'

We miss the pounding magnificence of love
and loving…for it 'fills' all spaces with its
glorious energies, its radiance…shall we accept it…
shall our souls climax within its magnificent splendor?

The answers are captured within, they are hidden in our
containment…loving can be "an extractor"
of the soul's solidifying power…to feel is to '*excess* 'in it.
Be not afraid of loving, for loving ecstasy
catapults us to 'the steaming heart.'

Bare the transcendence of the earth's love,
bare the joyous connection of unconscious passions, the
tender unseen *bounding* loving rhythms of *all* sensual expressions ….

Feel the opulence of those eternally connected feelings…
separation is death, connection is the 'perfect' source of light,
and its *loving* expansion.

We dwell to long in limited hard-covered containers, and experience
with life brings us there…doesn't it?

Follow the shadows and lines in Rodin's undivided lovers,
understand his intermixing of transitional loving ecstasy…and 'light'
…the power of this great joy can and will flow within you…
dance it!

And so two lovers lay exhausted in 'the magnificence' of their
ecstatic and 'heated' journey…never to wake…absorbed….

S.R. Dreben, 3/8/15

Ah, Beauty

Abound she was, exquisite in many ways…
She turned heads, caused *stirring* fascination in most quarters…
Sculpted features, perfectly tanned skin, legs, hands, torso all were exigent contributions to the exotic…

Voice, expressions, contours, poise, manners, style and grace…all encapsulated in this requisite beauty…and her hair sleek and auburn touching gracefully on the edges of her shoulders…contained and desired…always a saintly esoteric quality *pervades*…So, she dances in fragrant classy sensuality and grace…ah, one could only imagine her company…

And then the dinner, this long table with all the finery…elegance in food and drink…She sat at table's end without voice in dulled splendor…exposed as the limited icon she represented.

Years passed as her stature faded, dimmed like frosted light passing into a prairie of drought…desert now from years without rain. Hallowing reflections of great beauty past, scratching old portraits once there…and the quick disappearing continued until the skin released its hold. All chiseling vanished, so she searched through photos of rumpled ancient reflections long past…

And time came, and her bones blended with the dust of black space… her appearance dissolved and mixed…

"Ah, Beauty"

S.R. Dreben, 7/12/15

Collective Dream: 1945

Seemed only as a flash in a dream
until the winds blew, and the rain stained
the cedar porch with its tarry ooze.

Sadako woke slowly hearing screams from a distance
and then *silence* where voices once cried...

She was just nine, yet her life was always filled with flower
and craft...her father a master-cabinet maker trained in
centuries old techniques...everywhere was the striking beauty
of cherry wood...One could usually smell it...not this day.

Sadako Suzuki knew Origami paper crafts, her grandfather Akuro
taught her, they played with *paper folds* together as she grew...

She especially loved the white cranes, her designs won awards
she had a special touch, her fingers worked the cross folds
'so well'...

So, that day she envisioned cranes flying through dark rains
making their journey to safer places...better homes.

So, at nine she began folding her 'loving paper cranes'...until
she folded two hundred, then she slept.

Another day she folded another two hundred, her goal was one
thousand cranes, something which came to her in images.

Her body remained whole on the outside...yet...so many winds
blowing and blackened rains pounding the rooftops. She folded

cranes for another year, until her hands refused to fold another...

She constructed six hundred and forty-four cranes, and then
the sickness took her with the last cranes folded...

The children that were left loved her and folded the final paper cranes
until they reached a thousand structures...
a thousand snowy paper cranes
folded to perfection.

At every ceremony in Nagasaki for the next 68 years,
a Sadako paper crane was brought to the memorial
for all the beautiful beings taken in the *horror*.

Sadako Suzuki made the most graceful cranes ever presented
at the memorial...her folded paper designs filled the garden grounds
with an enormous peaceful LIGHT,
a crane for Nagasaki...her cranes for the lost...

*Regarding a Japanese Legend Sadako Suzuki,
who folded the white cranes...

S.R. Dreben, 8/9/15

...In Blood

Seeping into ...mosaics cracking with Age
dark reds...of torn bodies...laying on streets of frigid cold
...or the blistering summer's sun...

This bloody flesh and muscle just part of...
a veiled 'ritual sacrifice' of systematic elimination...

...So, in Syria, Iraq, Paris, Chicago, Ivory Coast,
New York, Baltimore, Nigeria...

Names in blood are 'imprinted' and departed
in never-ending reporting cycles...and most of it passes by in a glaze...
Crawford, Garner, Gray, Roberts...

Lamumba, Rice, Al Navir, Murat, Lincoln and Socrates...
fallen in 'contorted unison'...rendered indiscernible through
the arching keyholes of centuries...and we but surrender
to the ever-present shadows of selfishness, greed and forgetting...
laughing and clowning as we imbibe...indeed!

Whose blood is it, what meaning lies within these saturated currents;
too much...blood spilled...and I but an inchoate witness cries out...
no more...no more if it...

NO Bloody MORE!!

S.R. Dreben, 1/15/16

Nature & Time

A Millennium Tale

They were ancient travelers from a time when most northern coasts were frozen…moving on hallowed out wooded canoes, boats carved with ancient skills taken from the deeply frozen tundra of Northern Asia…those ancient tough coasts of the extreme north.

They fished with flint spearheads and small woven nets, they could stay alive because they melded with the frozen jagged places they continued crossing without fear…

Some nights they felt afraid, where polar bears, wolves, and grizzlies roamed freely…and sometimes the bowels of great walruses bellowed, stirred during mating…yet, *they* were part of it all…they were the new travelers in a rugged unknown…

As they moved southward down western North American coasts, *they* found abundance everywhere…the planet…nature itself led them, and in time they reached wetter places, where even greater **sustenance** was available…it was everywhere, pure and robust...and life flowered wondrously, to be seen, eaten, inhaled and touched. Nowhere were *they short* of anything…

Earth provides...and because of that humans continued traveling and growing, they spread their clans, their breed everywhere expanding without qualm and with little resistance...except for the storms...always the squalls, winds, rains and snows, fires and freezes eliminating *some* travelers and yet *some* always moved on...

So, they settled, hunted and fished, and even a few planted...most lived off the earth, and for thousands of years it continued...pristine water, food and air...all provided.

Ah, that was then...now is now...*few* can live this way again, as forests shrink, fish dwindle, species disappear rapidly, and acid from designer chemicals swirl their toxic mix in earth's skies and waters...

SHE cannot support us, she cannot fortify those that kill her, those that make her sick...the **indigenous** are the last ones, and they know... four more world peace prayer gatherings for Mother Earth, four more times...sixteen more years...

She is wounded, she is dying, she will turn it all over; yet in time she will return...when once again all is erased...except her...**she has time**, yet *they* may come once again, the *canoe roamers* may return...one more time...yet another time!!!

S.R. Dreben, 7/18/15

Old Friends

We gripped hands and felt the majestic current of source
...so many years passing without 'tension...'

No games whatever...few conflicts unresolved...

We who had *fully discovered* time together
...never waited for reply...we knew the levels,
we knew the script...we praised the pulse...

As time moved on 'the grip' became 'tighter'
automatic connections of exquisite understanding...feelings.

During a final walk in the greenery of early spring
some dew formed at the tip of our noses...strange
combinations of weather and breath...we laughed at each other
regarding these humorous images...

And then the quiet came...a closeness beyond silence...
somehow touching could be better than words...yes...?

Yet, all had deep extensions to the *intimate*...
a place where true friends may dwell forever without grief...

S.R. Dreben, 3/13/16

Nobody

After a while you forget the smells of the street...
you are one with it,
you and the 'other campers' accept the fragrance...

They are the nobodies...
and you are ...*Nobody.*
When you touch yourself, you feel nothing...
you are nobody...never forget that....

You search for nothing but survival...
and as the days and years pass you discover less....

Nobody is your brand, no one sees you,
few care as you walk along until the caverns and culverts welcome you...
you live nowhere, and you ARE nobody....

By Poet Steve Dreben //February 2017
Honorable Mention Oregon Poets Association Contest 'New Poets' 2016

The Dancer

She glided across the floor,
moved in perfect rhythm like a Cheetah forward to prey.
Then music filled the room, her sleek body "confronted us"
internal genuflections via muscular perfection…externally crafted.…

We…we were allowed a place…
a place where absolution, commitment and connection meet…
where stunning sculpted arms reached for the sun,
spinning and leaping to the driving pulses of "The Rites of Spring."

Caught in her spell…we gazed at her as she spun and twisted,
in one direction and another…
rapidly she danced with the speed of a champion boxer …
speeded coordination…in an exquisite unction of canonized rhythms…
"and time stops."

Colored lights followed her,
followed her prancing between light and shadow…
springing like a retreating Gazelle.…

As the beat pushed her…straining her very soul…
within and without a muscular canopy.

The purity of her shapely form extending again and again…
sweat pouring from her forehead…she danced like a Sultan's Goddess…
trained from childhood, picked to express spiritual perfection …
a studied physical prayer exhibiting life's fulfillments.

Her dance seemed beyond knowing,
and so we fell into 'silent space' …and this she allowed us.…

For several moments, *the dancer* was life…was both water and flame…
was the first moments of eternal spring…
and "we" the viewers of her dynamic prayer….

She sprang and dove, hand gestures giving us 'glimpses' of living,
glimpses of life worth living…a life woven precisely.

To be so close to a master of masters…
to feel her muscular visualizations and compressional movements. .
to be allowed the wondrous thrill of these meshing rhythms…
"a newly discovered life form."
As she spins and flowers like a song of the divine…
life's dance forever being reborn….

To be present, to be near this sweating passionate heart…
near this master…glistening human skin. …
A glacial experience within life's creation …
souls crying to be born. …

She stops, lights dim, music ceases…
yet the downpouring in each of us continues, it beats on!…
A wonderful sound…do you hear it?

S.R. Dreben, 12/09/12